ECSTASY

Also by Sudhir Kakar

ECSTASY

SUDHIR KAKAR

THE OVERLOOK PRESS
WOODSTOCK & NEW YORK

*To the memory of my father Sardarilal Kakar,
a confirmed agnostic,
and my mother Bimla, an equally convinced believer.*

First published in the United States in 2002 by
The Overlook Press, Peter Mayer Publishers, Inc.
Woodstock & New York

WOODSTOCK:
One Overlook Drive
Woodstock, NY 12498
www.overlookpress.com
[for individual orders, bulk and special sales, contact our Woodstock office]

NEW YORK:
141 Wooster Street
New York, NY 10012

Copyright © 2001 by Sudhir Kakar

♾ The paper used in this book meets the requirements for paper
permanence as described in the ANSI Z39.48-1992 standard.

Library of Congress Cataloging-in-Publication Data

Kakar, Sudhir.
Ecstasy / Sudhir Kakar.
p. cm.
1. Mystics—Fiction. 2. Aged men—Fiction. 3. Young men—
Fiction. 4. India—Fiction. I. Title
PR9499.3.K273 E28 2002   823'.914—dc21   2002022874

Manufactured in the United States of America
FIRST EDITION
ISBN 1-58567-210-6
1 3 5 7 9 8 6 4 2

ecstasy. The state of being 'beside oneself';
An exalted state of feeling which
engrosses the mind to the exclusion
of thought; rapture; transport

—*Oxford English Dictionary*

Gopal

I feel like dancing
The beat comes from you
Like a puppet on a string
You make me swing

—TUKARAM, *Tuka Says*

Chapter One

Gopal's visions ended when he grew breasts.

He was fifteen. His were not the flabby breasts of an old man but the small, firm and perfectly pronounced ones of a young girl. He had always been a plump child but now the loose flesh on his chest had gathered itself neatly into two distinct little mounds. For a while in the beginning, he kept the upper half of his body covered with a wrap even in the heat of summer. Sometimes, when he was alone in the fields, he would slap his breasts, saying, 'Go in, go in!'

There were other changes in his body. His genitals, too, were thickening, and grew darker than the rest of his skin. His shoulders broadened, but so did his hips, which again had a distinct swell to them. At the time he felt that his ecstatic states had ended because the gods had withdrawn from him since he was no longer a child, that they did not like the ways in which his body was changing.

Ever since he was ten years old, Gopal had been in great demand at religious ceremonies and festivals in the village, where he loved to sing in praise of whichever god or goddess was being celebrated. What so attracted his listeners was not only his sweet voice—a lyric soprano—or his ear for melody and rhythm, but the intensity and depth of feeling he put into his songs, especially those in praise of Krishna, his favourite god. It was as if he was in a trance. There were three occasions when sitting in front of the congregation, singing along with the others, he had seen the idol of the god come alive. Involuntarily, he had stood up and stretched his arms toward the deity. While an awed hush fell on the gathering, his body began to sway rhythmically as songs of praise came to his lips from somewhere deep within him, without his having made a conscious choice of a particular song or an effort to remember its words. The ecstatic mood deepened as he sang, and tears of joy streamed down his face from his half-closed eyes. After a while, the rapture was so sublime that his song stopped in mid-sentence. His limbs stiffened, his body became as rigid as a statue and he had to be supported by others lest he fell and hurt himself.

He was almost fourteen when he was graced with the last and most striking vision of his boyhood. It was early in the evening, at the beginning of the monsoon when the storm clouds have not yet covered the heavens in one dark, turgid mass but are still small and playful, jostling each other across an indulgent sky. He was returning home, munching on puffed rice, walking on a narrow mud embankment between the ploughed fields, when looking up he saw a flock of white cranes fly in an arc against an ink-black cloud that was rolling in to blot out the setting sun. The contrast in forms was so beautiful that he was filled with wonder and sank to the ground on his knees. And even as he went down, a tremendous force pulled him off the ground and placed him in the picture he had just seen. The cloud and the cranes curved in to enclose him and fill his entire vision. The clods of ploughed earth in the fields and the scarecrow made of dried millet stalks standing a few yards to his left disappeared. He felt he could almost touch the cloud, push his hand through the sliver of crimson light lining its edges. He could smell the coming rain, feel the cool breeze that was about to blow, and his feet tingled in anticipation of contact with wet earth.

Then the outer edge of his vision began to darken. The cloud and the cranes were swallowed up by the spreading darkness, which deepened for an infinitesimal moment before the sudden emanation of an inner light, as if in a rapidly accelerated dawn, that illuminated his whole field of vision. What he now beheld was Lord Krishna's blue-black chest with a garland of white jasmines thrown across its broad expanse. The invitation to rest his head against the Lord's dark flesh was irresistible, and as his cheek brushed against the dusky skin, ecstasy surged through his limbs in such a powerful current, filling him with a rapture so sublime, that he no longer knew himself to be in the body.

When he came back to the world that evening—he had not been unconscious but only absent, ecstatically absent—he found himself at home, lying on the familiar straw mat spread on the mud floor of the hut where he lived with his mother. A kerosene lamp burnt in one corner, throwing flickering shadows of his mother and the two squatting men on the wall in front of him. His head nestled in his mother's soft lap. The upper part of her body rocked back and forth as she made short, mewling sounds of distress. The two farmers who had found him lying in the field, apparently unconscious, and carried him home were vainly trying to reassure her that there was nothing wrong with the boy, that he had only fainted. When she saw him open his eyes, she gathered up his head in her arms and pressed it to her heart. Weeping uncontrollably with relief, she kissed him all over his face.

Amba worried about her son. Deeply religious herself, she welcomed Gopal's enthusiastic participation in her daily worship of the household gods but was torn about letting him go to the rituals of the neighbours. She did not think it was normal for a boy his age to be so religious and frowned when the village women told her that he was a singularly blessed child. 'O Gopal's mother,' they said, 'we are animals unless we sing to the Lord. Surdas says that to come to the feet of the Lord in song is enough to make stones float on the sea, and your son has been graced by God to touch Him through the realm of song. He is destined to be a great saint, like Surdas or Kabir.' Amba did not like this talk about saints.

'Saints leave home,' she had snapped back to one particularly tiresome neighbour. 'They never earn enough to support their families. May my Gopal's enemies become saints!'

The ecstatic trances had troubled her deeply. They were the province of hysterical young women or of God-crazed sadhus high on ganja, not of young boys. She suspected an undiagnosed physical malady behind the trances and his fainting in the fields that evening seemed to confirm her worst fears. She decided to keep him back from school till the Western-style doctor who came to Deogarh once in three weeks all the way from Jaipur, thirty miles away, had given the boy a thorough physical examination. She did not quite trust the village vaid, reputed to be a secret tippler of some of his own medicines which had a high proportion of alcohol in their base. He had found nothing wrong with the boy.

'You are blessed, Gopal's mother,' he had said, his breath reeking of alcohol and medicinal herbs, his yellow teeth spreading out crookedly in what was meant to be a winning smile. 'The boy's trances come from God, not from a disturbance in his bodily humours.'

Amba was impatient with the vaid not only because he was talking of trances and sainthood. It seemed to her that he was being dismissive about the illness because Gopal was a boy, and these men expected boys to be tough and hardy. Did the vaid not know that her Gopal was special? He was not like the other boys.

Gopal was indeed different. With his clear, lustrous skin, long eyelashes and delicate features, Gopal had always looked like a pretty girl, and the other boys had tormented him with coarse remarks and indecent gestures which made his eyes sting with hot tears of shame. Sometimes, when a boy had been especially obscene, a vile-tasting yellowish liquid—the physical expression of disgust in a pure soul—rose up in Gopal's throat, making him gag. Then one day, driven beyond the limits of endurance, the normally timid and gentle Gopal had cursed one of his tormentors, 'May a snake bite you as you sleep tonight. May you be dead by the morning. This is a Brahmin's curse, and a Brahmin's curse is a command even the gods dare not disobey.' The boys had fallen silent, their faces troubled. A Brahmin's curse was serious business, even if the Brahmin was a mere boy. The object of Gopal's wrath had tried to hide his unease but the exaggerated swagger he attempted as he turned and walked away betrayed his fear.

Nothing happened to the boy for a few days although he spent a couple of sleepless nights in the beginning. Then a week later, as he was dozing one afternoon under the shade of a mango tree, he was stung by a scorpion and fainted with pain. For the other boys, Gopal's curse had indeed come true and they avoided him after this incident. Wary of his demonstrated Brahmin prowess to successfully curse a tormentor, they stopped taunting him openly about the breasts and the female cast to his body. Instead, they exchanged knowing smiles and smirks whenever they saw him. As soon as he had walked past them and his back was turned, he heard them titter and occasionally imitate the outraged squeals of a girl whose breasts have been fondled by some ruffian. He hated all boys.

Gopal was not unduly put out by his isolation from the other boys. He preferred to be with women anyhow. He liked to accompany his mother when she went to the village well in the morning to fetch water and exchange gossip with other women. He loved to trudge behind her as she swept the floor of the hut. He was happy to cut the vegetables while she cooked and to scrub the cooking pot with water and clay after they had eaten. The morning and evening pujas, when he sang together with his mother, were the highlights of his day.

In the evenings, when the village had settled in for the night, the daytime sounds of birds, cattle and people replaced by the occasional barking of a dog and the distant screech of an owl, Gopal would lie next to his mother on the sleeping mat, still wide awake. He needed to talk, or rather hear the soothing murmur of her 'Hmm-m-ms' and monosyllabic replies that kept the darkness at bay, before he could let go of wakefulness. He wanted to chatter about all that had happened to him during the day, to pour out his love for her in the warmth of his voice and the fluttering touch of his fingers. It was only after he had revealed all the inconsequential secrets of a little boy's heart that he could fall asleep. All through the night, he slept with his body pressing tightly into his mother's back, the feel of her flesh imprinted on his own, its texture like a tattoo under his skin.

As a child Gopal's interactions with other women had something of the ease and comfort he felt with his mother. But over the last couple of years, he had begun to be wary of the village women who wanted him to sing in their pujas. The younger ones would ask him to sing of Radha's longing for Krishna and then whisper to each other and giggle while he sang. They touched him, too. Feathery, light brushes of their fingers on his groin from which he recoiled as if they were lances pressing into his skin. The older women were worse. He still revelled in the glow in their eyes when they sat across him in their kitchens, plying him with food. But he hated it when they pressed him to their breasts in an excess of adoration. He dreaded those moments when, suddenly, he would find a woman's arms flung around his neck and his face pulled violently forward, his nose squashed against soft flesh. He would struggle to turn his face away, to free his nose and mouth in order to breathe fresh air instead of the odour of sweat mixed with the smells of turmeric and fried onions.

'My Gopal,' the woman would cry out, oblivious to his discomfort, smothering him again and again in her billowing flesh as he struggled against drowning in it. The only way to escape was to push the woman away and then, to disguise the affront, shut his eyes and sing. The woman would draw back and listen then, controlling her impulse to embrace him tightly, while through the song Gopal escaped into the realm of the divine which was already his second home.

Chapter Two

The Vishnu temple at the top of the hill overlooking Deogarh had been built by Seth Lodhamal, of the same Bania family that had endowed Gopal's village with its school. Originally planned to rival the grand temples built in the villages of Shekhawati by other famous Bania migrants to Calcutta such as the Birlas, the Deogarh temple looked as if in the final phases of its construction its builder had suffered a massive haemorrhage either in his finances or in his faith. Indeed, Lodhamal had had to cut back on the construction costs after he lost heavily in speculation when jute prices collapsed at the end of the War. The dome of the temple and the pillars in the main hall were thus made of common sandstone rather than the gleaming white Makrana marble Lodhamal had originally intended to use. The temple's woodwork, too, was of cheap deodhar and not stately teak; and its flooring was laid with slate from unknown quarries rather than finished with the warm, honey-coloured stone tiles from Jaisalmer. The temple had looked shabby even at the time of its consecration.

During Gopal's boyhood, the temple lay deserted for most of the year. Devotees from Deogarh and some of the neighbouring villages visited it only on grand occasions, such as the birthdays of the great gods, especially Rama and Krishna. For their daily worship and festivities connected with the local and ancestral deities, each caste preferred to use their own modest temple in the village, or, in the case of the lowest castes, an open air shrine.

At the bottom of the hill was a rest house, attached to the Vishnu temple, for pilgrims and sadhus. Also a legacy of Lodhamal, it had been completed before the merchant lost most of his money, so there had been no compromise on quality. It was a pleasant, airy place with a sweet-water well rare in this sandy region, and had acquired a reputation among sadhus as a non-denominational resting place where ascetics of all sects were welcome. The reason for the popularity of this rest house was not the unremarkable Vishnu temple but the fact that it lay close to the pilgrim routes to a number of sacred sites: the temple of Sitalamata—the goddess of small pox—in Sheel Dungari; Naraina, the seat of the Dadupanth order of ascetics; the sun temple overlooking the Galta valley near Jaipur; and Pushkar and other sites even further south.

A couple of years after the Vishnu temple had been consecrated, Deogarh's residents became accustomed to the sight of all manner of sadhus, in varying states of sartorial splendour, walk through the bazaar on their way to the rest house. Some wrapped their bodies in unstitched white cloth. Others wore flowing ochre robes. Yet others preferred to go around naked except for a strip of faded red cloth that barely covered their genitals.

Gopal was fascinated by the sadhus. Even as a young boy

he would often wander up to the rest house and spend hours there, watching the awe-inspiring men who were so unlike the men of his village. The sadhus never objected to his presence. He was full of questions, and they answered them patiently. It did not take Gopal long to learn the distinguishing marks of the various orders of ascetics, happily communicating his discoveries to his mother when he returned home in the evenings from the rest house. The largest number of the sadhus belonged to one or the other of the ten Dashnami orders. They generally wore ochre, carried a single-pronged wooden staff and had a necklace of fifty-four rudraksha beads hanging around their necks. The horizontal markings on their foreheads, reverently drawn every morning with ash, were either the three lines representing the trident of Shiva or just two lines, with a dot above or below to symbolize his phallus.

The followers of Vishnu preferred to wear white, often shaved their heads—in contrast to the matted locks sported by many Dashnamis—and wore a necklace of basil beads. Like the Dashnamis they too were further subdivided into different monastic orders. The worshippers of the combined image of Sita and Rama could be recognized by their necklaces of one hundred and eight basil beads, the three-pronged staff they carried, and the two white and one red vertical lines on their foreheads. The worshippers of Radha and Krishna had a U-shaped white or black forehead marking and wore a string with a single large basil bead around their necks.

Within each monastic order, every sadhu occupied a specific place in the hierarchy according to his level of spiritual attainment—from the novice through the Avadhoot to the most highly evolved of all, the Paramahamsa. Of the latter, Gopal was told, there were no more than a dozen in the land. The greatest Paramahamsa of the last one hundred years, some said, was the saint Ramakrishna of Dakshineshwar, although others disputed this claim.

A Paramahamsa, Gopal learnt, was a person who was so far advanced on the spiritual path and had attained such a deep knowledge of the Self that the routine observances enjoined on the ascetic, such as vegetarian food, were no longer binding on him. If most Paramahamsas continued to be vegetarians it was out of choice.

'Unlike the rest of us,' one sadhu said, 'the Paramahamsa chooses what he must.'

'Ah!' said another, adding to Gopal's confusion, 'he may do as he likes only because he does not do what he wants.'

The sadhus took childish delight in making such cryptic pronouncements which Gopal found baffling at the time and did not understand till he was much older.

'How will I recognize a Paramahamsa?' the boy once asked.

'You will see him with your spiritual eyes when the time is ripe,' was one unsatisfactory answer.

'You could pass him in the bazaar and never know him for one,' another sadhu explained. 'He can behave like a madman although he is the sanest of men, the supreme discriminator who has realized the identity of the individual self with that of the Universal Soul.

'His self-control is so perfect that nothing can disturb his equanimity—unless, of course, he chooses to be disturbed.

He is so pure that the most polluting of substances cannot soil his purity. He is the follower of Shiva or Vishnu or both. He is a monist or a theist or neither. He believes in a personal God or in a God without form and qualities or does not speak of God at all.'

'Don't confuse the poor boy,' an old sadhu who had just joined the group said. 'Listen, son. One day my brother's five-year-old grandson was trying to catch grasshoppers near the pond outside our village. A strong breeze was blowing. To stop the leaves from rustling, he addressed the tree. "Hush!" he said. "I want to catch a grasshopper." Another day it was quite stormy and there were flashes of lightning. Peeping out of the window, he announced to the family, "Look! They are striking matches again!" So, son, a Paramahamsa is like this five-year-old boy all the time. He sees everything filled with consciousness.'

That evening, while sitting in front of the cooking fire, eating his dinner, Gopal asked his mother, 'Can I become a Paramahamsa, maa? I would like to be one.'

She did not answer immediately as she ladled more dal onto his brass plate. He had always been such a sweet child, with a gentle innocence that had not left him even now that he was older and on the verge of youth. Except for his abnormal interest in religious matters and the time he did not want to go to school because of the cruelty of other boys, he had never given her cause for concern. The fate that had deprived her of a husband at such a young age had also blessed her with a son whose world revolved around his mother. She could not imagine them ever being parted.

'I only want my Gopal, not a Paramahamsa,' she said

lightly although her heart was heavy with foreboding.

The village of Deogarh where Gopal grew up in the early 1930s lay thirty miles north of Jaipur. Spread out at the foot of a low, rocky hill covered with dry scrub and a sparse jungle, Deogarh was a fairly large habitation of about two hundred households. The majority of the men were tenant farmers, with small holdings, rarely more than fifteen acres, which they leased from the Maharaja of Jaipur, the *durbar*. They grew two crops a year: wheat in winter and maize in summer; and had enough to eat if the rain-god, well known for his capricious nature in this part of the country, was favourably inclined. The vagaries of the gods, however, were as nothing compared to the greed of powerful men.

Whenever the rains were insufficient, a not infrequent occurrence in these dry parts, the villagers borrowed money at exorbitant rates of interest from the moneylenders. Even in good times, they did not hesitate to borrow on special family occasions such as weddings when honour, especially among the Rajputs, demanded that these be extravagantly celebrated by spending money one did not have. The result was that after each harvest the moneylender and the revenue collector for the durbar got together to decide how much of his produce a farmer needed to surrender in order to satisfy them both and have enough to survive. Inevitably, this share was much larger than the one half of the harvest that the durbar had fixed as land revenue.

Compared to the thakurs and other petty chieftains of his

kingdom, though, the Maharaja of Jaipur was a positively benevolent landlord. The thakurs levied a cess on every possible celebration they could think of: birthdays of the chief and his heir, birthdays of the gods, palace weddings, births and deaths. Even the frequent hunting trips which the Rajput barons loved were paid for by levying a tax on the peasants. When a special British guest and his *mem* who had motored down from Delhi set out with the baron and his retainers on a hunt, they were seldom aware that the expenses for the expedition, including the lavish meals washed down with bottles of Scotch whisky and fine French wines, were being borne by the undernourished men with large turbans and spindly legs who prostrated themselves in the dust by the side of the road as the elephants bearing the hunting party passed by.

The result of such widespread exploitation was that except for a few *bhumiya* Rajputs who still owned their patrimonial lands, the other cultivators were little more than serfs, held to rather than holding their lands. It was a hard life, and it had been so for centuries.

Deogarh, then, like so many other villages around Jaipur, was not a very prosperous village. A dusty lane, starting from the bottom of the hill, ran through the middle of the village— where it became the bazaar—and then out through the fields to join the Delhi-Jaipur highway, five miles away. Lined on each side with shops of grain and cloth merchants, and a number of smaller shops selling brass and copper utensils, oil, tea, salt, cakes of jaggery and other household goods, the bazaar was the common meeting ground and centre of gossip for the whole village. Emaciated cattle and stringy goats strayed through it on their way to graze at the slope of the hill. Often camels would be ridden through the bazaar or tethered in front of the tea shops while their owners stopped for a tumbler of hot, milky tea and a couple of drags at the long-stemmed *hukkah*.

The bazaar also served as the weekly market for half-a-dozen surrounding villages. Gopal often went to the bazaar on market days when it was crowded with visitors. He especially liked to watch large family groups moving noisily from one shop to another. The women in colourful *ghagra-cholis* and the children dressed as little adults went about in tight clusters. And the tall, gaunt men, in their faded white tunics but wearing glorious red, magenta, yellow and piercingly pink turbans, walked at the periphery of these groups. With the intent, watchful expressions of sheep dogs, they herded any child along who lingered too long in front of a shop. They were more patient with their women while they bargained for small luxuries—coloured glass bangles for themselves, a piece of cloth for a child's shirt, gnarled turmeric roots and dried red chillies for the kitchen and, perhaps after an especially bounteous harvest, a burnished copper pot and new brass tumblers for the family.

On either side of the bazaar, narrow alleys led into clusters of closely packed houses with mud-plastered stone walls and tiled roofs. The layout of the village had a precise order not immediately apparent to the casual observer. The clusters of houses were divided into three sectors, each the home of a major caste group—Rajput, Bania and Jat—the crooked boundaries between the sectors as clear cut as they were invisible. These three enclaves were the largest pieces in the mosaic that was Deogarh, and the inhabitants of each enclave had their own preferred gods, customs, traditions and lifestyles, though they also shared much, including gods and festivals, that was the common heritage of the village.

Further down, toward the outskirts, were the mud-walled, thatched huts of the humbler communities— the agricultural labourers and the cowherds, the barbers and the cobblers, the two blacksmiths, and the oil presser in whose courtyard a blindfolded ox circled all day around a wooden press. The eight Brahmin households, Gopal's among them, which provided the village with its priests as well as its genealogist and its school teacher, were bunched in a separate enclave of their own near that of the Rajputs who were the dominant caste.

Because of their clan links with the barons of the area, and indeed the Maharaja of Jaipur, the Rajputs had a great sense of pride and claimed higher social status. The hard-working and the much thriftier Jats, also small cultivators, now contested this claim. The Jat children had begun to go to school. The Rajputs, on the other hand, following the example of their chiefs who considered reading and writing arts they paid their servants to perform for them, disdained all academic education. In the mid-1930s, when Gopal was in his early teens, the increasing animosity between the Jats and the Rajputs had come to a head, threatening to erupt in a riot between the two communities that had the potential to spread to large areas of Rajputana. It had all begun with Bhawani Singh and the wedding horse.

Bhawani Singh was a hot-headed young Rajput, a picture-book reproduction of Rajput manhood, who served in the Maharaja of Jaipur's cavalry, the Kachwaha Horse. He had a young bride waiting at home, but his visits to the village were rare. Feted and fawned upon by other young Rajputs when he did come, Bhawani Singh spent most of his time in the village drinking with his friends. They flattered him with their attentiveness and he regaled them with accounts of court intrigues and other gossip from the capital city.

On one of his visits to Deogarh, Bhawani Singh was returning home at night with one of his drinking friends when they encountered a Jat wedding procession on the way. The two Rajputs stood to one side to let the wedding party pass through the narrow lane. Even in his drunken state Bhawani Singh registered the fact that the bridegroom was riding a horse. This was unheard of, an outrage to all decent sentiment. Jats were forbidden to ride horses, a privilege reserved only for the Rajputs.

'Bastards!' Bhawani Singh shrieked and then ran home to fetch the family sword, a reminder of the community's glorious warrior past. Minutes later, he reappeared and rushed toward the horse brandishing the sword. Before he could do any damage, he was felled by the blow of a bamboo stock to his head. Enraged young Jats hit him on the head a couple of times more before they were pulled back by the elders of the community. The unconscious Bhawani Singh was brought home by his parents who had tried in vain to stop him. He died in the morning without regaining consciousness.

The tension in the bazaar of Deogarh was palpable that morning. It hung heavy in the wintry air, seeping into the cold eyes of grim-faced men and the hurried movements of women anxious to reach the safety of their homes. In the Rajput quarter, young men were taking down swords and spears from hooks on the walls where these ancient weapons of war had long hung unused. An armed clash with the Jats seemed imminent. In the adjoining Brahmin enclave, Amba would not allow her son to leave the hut. Those men would turn the village into a battlefield; she could not let her son walk out alone, seeking the company of the sadhus.

The expected riot between the Rajputs and the Jats never took place. The prompt arrival of a party of the durbar's armed police kept an uneasy peace in the village for the next two days, giving the hotheads of both communities a chance to cool down and the grey heads time to hammer out a settlement. The Jats finally apologized for Bhawani Singh's killing which the Rajputs acknowledged did not amount to murder. The Jats also agreed to pay a suitable compensation to the dead man's family and promised not to violate the old custom pertaining to the riding of a horse.

Deogarh's Brahmins remained neutral in this caste conflict, although as upholders of tradition their natural sympathy lay with the Rajputs. They were a small, close-knit community that had quickly rallied to the support of Amba and her son when Gopal's father, the hereditary astrologer of the village, died of tuberculosis when Gopal was five years old. Gopal's memories of his father were hazy but the picture of his mother on the day of the funeral was sharp and detailed. Amba sat stone-faced in the centre of a circle of weeping women. The vermilion powder in the parting of her hair had been wiped off, leaving a faint smear in the middle of her forehead. Her gold necklace and earrings lay heaped in a small pile in front of her. The vaid's wife was breaking Amba's glass bangles with a stone, erasing the last insignia of her married state, wailing piteously as she did so, mourning the loss of Gopal's father but also anticipating her own dreaded widowhood. Clinging to his mother, her warm flesh a bulwark against the feeling of inner disintegration and the wave of hopelessness that swept over him, Gopal, too, had wept along with the women. Amba was already dressed in the white sari she would wear for the rest of her days. Like the Banias and the Rajputs and unlike the Jats and other lower castes, Brahmin widows never remarried.

When Amba's two brothers came from Shekhawati to take her and the child back to their native village, the Brahmin community of Deogarh persuaded Amba to stay on and not return to her parents' home. 'Sister, we are as much your family as they are,' they said with a sincerity that proved to be surprisingly durable, outlasting the sentiment required by the sad occasion. With two quarrelsome sisters-in-law ruling the roost in her parents' home after her mother's death and a sick father who could no longer be a provider for his daughter and grandson, Amba thought it prudent to remain in Deogarh. The brothers, secretly relieved, went back professing eternal devotion and promising immediate help if it was ever needed.

The early death of Gopal's father had meant a considerable fall in their living standard but not a descent into penury. Gopal's grandfather, Pandit Vishnu Dutt Sharma, had been a renowned astrologer in his time. His reputation had even reached the durbar. Consulted on behalf of the ruler, Sawai Madho Singh, in the matter of the Dundlodh rebellion caused by the Maharaja installing his own man as ruler of that estate, Vishnu Dutt had foretold the surrender of the Rajput defenders of Dunlodh fort without any loss of life to the Maharaja's besieging army. Pleased by his accurate prediction, Madho Singh had rewarded the astrologer by granting him ten acres of good quality land. The land was now tilled by a Jat farmer and Gopal and his mother survived on the rent paid in kind. The other Brahmin families helped by marketing their share of the produce, negotiating with the revenue collector on their behalf and composing the occasional representation to the durbar petitioning a reduction in revenue.

In spite of being a poor widow, Gopal's mother was treated with respect in the village. For although the Brahmins of Deogarh were a miniscule minority, they were still part of the larger, powerful community of Brahmins in the state of Jaipur who served the Rajput princes and barons as their ministers and confidential servants, cooks and keepers of the wardrobe, astrologers and physicians, bards and genealogists.

The rest house had become Gopal's new school, and the peripatetic sadhus his teachers, who imparted to him, their sole pupil, the knowledge of the life of the soul. Indiscriminate in his awe and adoration, Gopal revered all sadhus. His mother cautioned him not to be taken in by appearances. There were always a few scoundrels among these men of God who, masquerading as renouncers of the world, were actually vagrants looking for free meals and leading dissolute lives full of drugs and drink. But with his overwhelming urge to adore rather than discriminate, Gopal could not but be oblivious to Amba's warnings.

Between the ages of thirteen and fifteen, the rest house became the focus of his life. After helping his mother with the household chores in the morning and then going to school, he spent most of his afternoons with the sadhus, returning home after the evening worship, well past sunset. His mother, who had always worried, showed her disapproval by waiting up for him and not eating the evening meal till he was back. But she had been brought up with the beliefs and rituals of an orthodox Brahmin family, and it was difficult for her to forbid her son to associate with the holy men whom she, too, had been taught to revere.

Gopal loved to hear the sadhus talk as they sat around in small groups, smoking ganja from a common *chillum*, exchanging information on the pilgrim centres where the best ganja was to be had, rich households on the pilgrim trails that were especially generous to wandering sadhus, and generally exchanging monastic gossip. Some also told tales of Yogic miracles and argued theological matters, using stories from the lives of saints and gods to illustrate the point they were making, the connection between the story and a particular argument growing weaker as the afternoon wore on and the drug took hold. It was with these sadhus that Gopal felt he was approaching an unseen world which was his real home, a world from which he had been exiled long ago, before the birth of memory, and which he had glimpsed in his rare ecstatic states.

Not that the sadhus were oblivious to Gopal's appearance or completely indifferent to his twin-gendered body. But when a sadhu looked at Gopal's breasts and hips with a show of interest, then the look was more in appreciation of the mystery lying at the heart of human life than of vulgar curiosity, a look of awe rather than scorn. Gopal had often heard them say that everything about the body—and, indeed, also the mind—was conditioned, plastic, impermanent . . . and thus false.

The sadhus' easy acceptance of the boy changed into astonished respect when they heard him sing during the evening worship. 'A born sadhu!' they exclaimed in wonder as his soul took wing and his melodious voice soared in praise. They vied with each other in imparting their knowledge to a young boy who was so obviously destined to scale great spiritual heights. They told him about the various stages in the spiritual journey a seeker undertakes with the help of Yogic practices and meditation. They told him about how the body becomes slowly spiritualized during the first stage: 'It feels light as the flesh takes on the pure poise of spirit. The voice becomes melodious, and the body's odour pleasant as the bodily wastes, urine and excreta, decrease markedly. In the advanced stages, in the first heaven of knowing, the adept has visions of gods and of marvellous other worlds, of the universe filled with sparks of fire or glittering like a lake of quicksilver. They are images full of conviction and clarity. The visions and other spiritual experiences are accompanied by such feelings of joy and exaltation that having once sampled their nectar the palate becomes indifferent to the tastes of ordinary life.'

The accounts of the spirit's progress fascinated Gopal less than the tales of miraculous powers, the *siddhis*, which a sadhu could acquire—or rather set free within himself—on the way to the spirit's perfection. As the meditation deepened, one not only began to perceive sounds, smells, tastes and colours that lay beyond the bounds of normal perception but could even create them. Gandha Baba of Benares, for instance, could give the perfume of any flower to a scentless one or make a person's skin exude a delightful fragrance without touching him. It was a scent that lingered for days and was perceptible to anyone who came near the person. An accomplished Yogi could read the thoughts of others and control their actions by a concentration of his will. He could liberate matter, both coarse and subtle, from its natural limitations, alter its atomic structure, and thus free his body and mind from all that would impinge upon them.

Of all the men of God Gopal met in the rest house, the one who later stood out in his memory—besides the tantrik who would transform his life—was Shivananda, a middle-aged man with a forbidding expression who generally kept to himself but who took a liking to the boy after he heard him sing. Shivananda often sought Gopal out during the week he stayed at the rest house, asking the boy to accompany him on his evening walk up to the Vishnu temple which he showed no inclination to enter. Once, after returning from the walk, they were sitting outside the rest house, the sadhu perched on the stone embankment enclosing the well and Gopal squatting at his feet, when

Shivananda was stung on the neck by a large, yellow black-bottomed wasp. Except for a momentary frown at the time of the sting there was no change in Shivananda's calm expression. He had developed the siddhi of 'fierce bliss' which converted pain into pleasure.

'Earlier, only dull kinds of pain had this quality,' he explained to the boy who was gaping at him in wonder, 'but now it has also extended to those which are acute. I don't know whether I could also thus convert an intense pain which goes on for a long time. Not like my guru.'

One day, while begging for his food, Shivananda's guru, who never wore clothes, had absent-mindedly entered the women's quarters of a Muslim grandee. Hearing the frightened screams of the women, the nobleman came rushing in and in his rage aimed a mighty blow of his sword at the nude guru's shoulder, severing his arm. The guru turned and quietly walked away. Realizing his error and overcome with remorse, the nobleman picked up the arm from the floor and hurried after the sadhu. When he caught up with the sadhu, he apologized profusely and handed back the severed limb. The guru thanked him politely and nonchalantly inserted the arm into the bleeding stump.

The next day, while they were walking on the path that led to the temple, Shivananda pointed to a young tree yet to grow to its full stature.

'Look at the squirrel on the trunk,' he said to Gopal. 'It will clamber up to the top branch. It will then come down the tree trunk and disappear behind that bush over there.'

With mounting astonishment, Gopal watched the squirrel exactly follow the predicted sequence of actions.

'I saw the first two motions in the squirrel's mind before they were executed and the last through the siddhi of directly seeing into the past, present and future,' Shivananda explained.

But in spite of his own siddhis, Shivananda remained singularly unimpressed by the matter of Yogic powers.

'Ha! Harnessing God to manufacture smells!' he had snorted when Gopal told him the story he had heard about Gandha Baba.

On another occasion, when Gopal excitedly asked whether the stories about Trailinga Baba who weighed over two hundred pounds although he hardly ate and who could stay underwater for hours or walk on air three feet above the ground were true, Shivananda was scornful.

'A frog is also at home in water. The crow and the vulture can both easily fly through air. Remember, what is important is to realize God, not such trifles.'

'But which god, Maharaj?' Gopal asked.

'There is only one—the Brahman without form who is venerated in several manifestations. Shiva, Rama, Krishna, Hanuman, Ganesha, Durga, Kali—they are all different forms of the same God. You can choose the one who arouses your deepest love. Worship that form as your Divine ideal. We are not like the Jews, Christians or Muslims who may love God only as the father—never as mother, son or lover. Imagine the blight on the spiritual life of someone who is unable to love God as the father, whose natural inclination is to establish a different relationship with the Divine. His worship will forever remain hollow, a mere shell of rituals without that emotional sap which makes a ritual come alive.'

Gopal was moved by the sadhu's eloquence, though he was not sure that he understood.

Chapter Three

Gopal was on his way back home from the festival ground at the outskirts of the village when he first met the tantrik. He had spent a most satisfying afternoon at the Teej celebrations which the other boys avoided because Teej was considered a women's festival. He had happily wandered among rickety wooden stalls that sold glass bangles and clay images of various gods and goddesses. He had gawked at the lurid poster tacked to the magician's tent which showed a lushly bearded man sawing a little girl in half, and, since he had no money, had easily resisted the temptation posed by the merry-go-round and the hawkers selling dried red berries and yellow sweets made from *gur* and *besan*. Groups of women dressed in the festival finery of ghagra-cholis and long *odhnis* draped over the head and tucked in at the waist, eddied all around him, resplendent in the sharp, bright colours of the desert dwellers. It made him feel safe and gave him a sense of freedom as heady as it was rare. He wished he could have stayed longer. For later in the evening the flares would be lit, sending streamers of dull yellow light sailing through the hazy darkness. The drums would begin to beat, summoning the women to the festival's climax—the Teej dance. But it was time for the evening worship at the rest house and the sadhus would be expecting him.

The celebratory mood was still upon him, quickening his steps as he walked back. When he reached a deserted stretch of the dirt road, he gave in to a sudden impulse and changed his walk to imitate that of a girl—left foot forward first, shoulders erect, hips swaying, neck held straight, as if carrying pitchers of water balanced on the head. He was so engrossed in the imitation that he did not hear the man come up behind him.

'How far to the rest house?' the man asked in a deep, clear voice.

Gopal looked up in embarrassment. The man's glittering eyes held his, and he found himself unable to lower his gaze or look away.

'I am going there myself, Maharaj,' he replied, the quaver in his voice slight but unmistakable.

The tantrik was a powerfully built man in his mid-thirties. A red cloth, faded to the colour of an old brick from many washings, was tied around his waist. A bag made from the same coarse material, containing his few worldly possessions, hung from his right shoulder. Rings of silver and gold, studded with semi-precious stones—turquoise, opal, aquamarine, garnet, moonstone, onyx—adorned most of his fingers. Large earrings made from rhinoceros horn dangled from holes in the hollows of his ears. A two-feet-long string made from black sheep's wool and with a single rudraksha bead hung around his neck. The upper half of his bare body and his legs were burnt to the colour of dark mahogany by the sun.

Combing back his shoulder-length curly hair with his bejewelled fingers—a rapid dance of pinpoints of light through a dark mass—the tantrik smiled at the boy. The smile was forced and pinched but still made his fierce black-bearded face slightly softer, less menacing. Tantriks were fearsome people, notorious for their occult powers, obscene rituals and complete lack of morals. One of their sects, Gopal had heard from the other sadhus, was so supremely indifferent to conventional morality and civilized practices that its members could even eat dung with all signs of enjoyment, and consumed human flesh whenever it was available, raking pieces of charred flesh from funeral pyres and digging up corpses from fresh Muslim graves.

'I shall walk with you then,' the tantrik said.

Gopal's unease lessened but did not disappear as the tantrik fell in step beside him and they seemed to walk companionably along, the man humming a song under his breath that Gopal could not quite place.

'How long will the Maharaj be with us?' Gopal asked.

'Water flows, the sadhu wanders,' replied the man.

It was near dusk, 'cow-dust time' in folk poetry, when a greyish-pink haze of dust stirred up by cattle returning after feeding in the scrub hangs in the air. It is a time of transition from day to the evening, marked by the ringing of bells in the temples and the lowing of cows. Just as the light of the sun is replaced by myriad small glows of cooking fires and lighted lamps, life in the public spaces of the village begins to fragment and retreat into the privacy of individual families.

As they left the path and turned into the gate of the rest house, the tantrik spoke again:

'Are you a boy or a girl?'

Before Gopal could stammer a reply, the man answered the question himself: 'Both. Neither.' And laughed the singular laugh of a man who is rarely able to smile.

'Be careful that your buttocks do not bulge out like the hind parts of black ants,' the tantrik continued in a teasing voice. 'Women with such buttocks are inordinately attached to sensual enjoyment.'

Gopal flushed with humiliation.

'The Goddess must have directed me to you,' the man said more kindly, ruffling Gopal's hair.

After an initial exchange of polite greetings, it was evident that the other sadhus were avoiding the tantrik. All conversation ceased whenever he came near a group. The squatting men seemed to hold their breath till he moved away, as if the smell of cremation grounds where some tantriks performed their abominable rituals still clung to his body. The tantrik appeared oblivious to their disregard. Throwing down his bag in one corner of the large hall where the sadhus slept on mats rolled out on the floor, he walked around the hall, as if inspecting the amenities, before he strode out to the well in the courtyard. Drawing up a bucket of water, he began to wash, rubbing himself vigorously under the arms and across his chest. He sang lustily as he bathed. Gopal now recognized the song the tantrik had hummed on the way. It was a song in praise of the goddess Kundalini, the cosmic energy that lies coiled like a snake at the base of the spine.

The tantrik did not join in the evening puja. But as he was singing the last bhajan, Gopal saw him come in and sit down

on the floor directly in front of him. In the dim light of the oil
lamp, his eyes seemed to be flecked with the metallic hue of
iron filings. His look was cold and piercing, like a spear in
Gopal's chest, and the boy felt a spasm of terror pass through
his body. His voice shook and then petered into silence. He
got up to leave, and felt the tantrik's stare rake his back as he
stumbled out of the rest house. A hot moon hung in the sky.
He was feverish by the time he reached home.

After many years, Gopal's nightmares returned that
night. As a child, his nights had been often disturbed by
frequent eruptions of frightening images into his sleeping
consciousness. The nightmares had been as much a part of
his childhood as the occasional visions that he desperately
longed for; the two playing on the same stage, separated by
the thinnest of screens. For two days, Gopal was unable to
leave his mother's side. He woke up when she did, just before
sunrise, and accompanied her to the fields. Here he waited at
the precise distance which would protect her modesty and at
the same time let him keep at least the top of her head in view
as she squatted among the wheat stalks to relieve herself.
Even a few minutes of her being away from home were
enough to produce such frightening sensations that he would
cry out in panic. During the day her absence opened the door
to a dark, overwhelming fear that rushed in to smother his
entire world, emptying it of all that was good. At night, the
smallest sound, the minutest changes of light and shade, the
quivering shapes of objects in the dark, all took on an air of
extreme menace which he felt would never end till his mother
returned and called out his name, her voice lighting up every
corner of the hut and his mind, sending the unknown dangers

scurrying away.

On the afternoon of the third day, Gopal's mother forced him to go out.

'Even to the rest house to your sadhus if you must, but go!' she said.

Gopal did not protest. He had begun to feel better since the morning, less anxious, not so fearful. He even looked forward to being with those men of God again, listening to their talk of Yogic powers and miracles and singing in the evening worship.

At the foot of the hill the man was waiting for him. The red cloth bag, from which a pair of iron tongs peeped out, was slung over a polished brown shoulder. In his right hand he was holding his begging bowl, a blackened coconut shell reminiscent of the upper half of the human skull members of the Aghori sect still carried with them.

'You didn't come for two days,' his tone was reproachful.

Gopal stiffened. Again, he stood transfixed in the tantrik's gaze. The man looked different today, more intense. His eyes no longer glittered but were more opaque, as if focussing inwards. In a way, it was even more unnerving to be looked at sightlessly. The afternoon began to tremble with an old fear.

'This is the last day of the year when the heavens are ruled by Mahadev in his form as the Lord-who-is-half-woman. I was waiting for you. At last I can worship Shiva in an idol which is not of stone but of a living flesh that partakes of both male and female natures,' the man said as he walked up the path, leading the way, confident that the boy would follow.

An old sadhu was the only one to be seen outside the rest house, washing his loin cloth at the well. He looked up incuriously as they walked past him, greeting them with a mumbled 'Jai Ram' before he bent down to haul up a bucket of water.

The temple at the top of the hill was deserted and the tantrik quickly strode through the central pillared hall to the courtyard at the back.

'Sit!' he commanded.

Gopal felt his will wholly subordinated to that of the man. He could not even lift a finger unless the tantrik told him to do so. The last traces of volition were leaving his mind as a feeling of utter surrender, at once exhilarating and fearful, took over. From a distance, much farther than the few feet separating them, he watched the tantrik take out the ingredients for worship from his cloth bag—black gobs of sweet-smelling resinous *dhoop*, a small earthen lamp with a cotton wick, a box of matches and a bottle of mustard oil.

'Take off your clothes,' the man said as he busied himself filling the lamp with oil and rolling the dhoop into finger-length lumps which he placed in a semi circle around the boy. A weak impulse of opposition, no more than a proto-thought of refusal, arose in the boy's mind, fluttered there weakly for a moment before it was crushed by the man's will. Obediently, he followed the order.

After lighting up the lamp and the dhoop which immediately began to emit thick curls of perfumed smoke, the man began to rub oil into the boy's body, beginning with the breasts and moving over to the shoulders and arms with long glides of his hands. After the first shock of a callused oily palm grating against his skin, Gopal did not feel anything at all. His limbs felt paralyzed, without sensation. Spells of nausea mingled with swirls of fading consciousness as the tantrik continued the massage, singing to himself as he did so. The last thing Gopal remembered before he slid into a state devoid of all memory was the sultry fragrance of the dhoop and the refrain of the song in the man's deep voice—'Awaken, O Mother! O Kundalini, whose nature is eternal bliss!'

Gopal would later remember coming awake, as if after a long, dreamless sleep, to the pungent odour of mustard oil, the feel of cold stone slabs against his skin and the sight of his crumpled clothes lying next to a still glowing lump of dhoop. As he tied his tunic and then pulled his shirt over his head, he felt a mixture of extraordinary sensations spread through his back. What the tantrik's puja had done, Gopal told his disciples many years later, was to awaken his Kundalini from where she slept at her seat above the anus. He had felt alternating currents of keen elation and piercing pain begin in his rectum and shoot up the rope of his spine. The latter were so painful that he had to contract his anal muscles tight to withstand the torture. The spontaneous movements of the Kundalini subsided after a few minutes, leaving behind a dull ache in his anus which persisted all the way home.

It would be many years before Mother Kundalini would once again awaken within Gopal, much more gently this time, and commence her stately journey up through his spine and the *chakras* to the realm of God-consciousness which he could now enter at will.

Vivek

Little by little, belief became polluted
like air and water.

—MICHEL DE CERTEAU,
The Practice of Everyday Life

Chapter Four

The early afternoon sun was unseasonably hot for late October. It had drained the sky of its morning azure, leaving behind the palest of blue. High above, a couple of eagles glided along its glazed surface in long, meandering arcs. The four boys sat under the shade of a pipal tree at the edge of the Maharaja College cricket ground. They were trying to reach a consensus on how to spend the rest of the afternoon. Nemi Chand and Suresh, both final year students of economics, were in favour of going down to M. I. Road and having tea and vanilla ice cream at Niro's. For Nemi Chand, 'tea at Niro's' was a euphemism for an order of fried fish and chips, forbidden food in his vegetarian Jain household. Kamal, a post-graduate student of physics, was decidedly against the spending of so much money. His suggestion, which he insisted had the merit of combining frugality with variety, was a leisurely bike ride through the Ramnivas Gardens and watching some cricket while munching on roasted peanuts. The afternoon outing was then to be concluded at Ganeshi Ram's stand in front of the museum, where they would quaff glasses of fresh sugarcane juice spiced with ginger and lemon.

Even as they talked, the three boys were waiting for

Vivek, a final year student of philosophy and the acknowledged leader of their small group, to express his preference.

'No, yaar,' Vivek finally spoke. 'All this is so boring. Let's do something very different.'

'What about cards in the hostel?' Suresh suggested. 'Bridge, I mean,' he amended hastily, disassociating himself from the non-stop three-card flush that went on in the student hostel during the whole of the academic year and stopped only at the onset of the long summer vacation.

Nemi Chand, whose suggestions generally limited themselves to 'tea at Niro's', came up with a surprise.

'Let us go and see Ram Das Baba. May be he'll get into one of his ecstasies.'

Seeing the expression of distaste on Kamal's face, he hastily added: 'He's not like the others, yaar. An uncle of mine swears the man is a great saint, a Paramahamsa like Ramakrishna or Ramana Maharishi.'

Ram Das Baba was a sadhu who had come to live in the Sitaram temple opposite Vidiadhar's garden around the same time the state of Jaipur became a part of independent India in 1949. That was sixteen years ago, when the sadhu was barely in his twenties. His reputation as a highly evolved spiritual being had soon begun to attract a large number of visitors to this small and otherwise undistinguished temple. He was renowned for his frequent *samadhi* states, for sojourning in the highest spiritual realms almost at will. He could be discoursing on a saint's love for the Divine or listening raptly to a devotional song by one of the disciples he had begun to gather around him when the ecstatic mood would suddenly overtake him. His body would become stiff while his half-closed eyes beheld rapturous visions which he sometimes described when he came out of his ecstatic trance.

'They are nothing but the hallucinations of a madman, yaar,' Kamal, the scion of minor Rajput nobility and the avowed Marxist of the group, protested against the suggestion.

'It's a good idea,' Vivek overruled him. 'We can have some fun with him on all this God-realization business. College is such a bore.'

Nemi Chand, who came from a family of devout believers, looked clearly uneasy but was too overawed by both Vivek and Kamal to protest at the shape their expedition was taking.

Wheeling out their bicycles from the college gate, the boys turned left on Sawai Man Singh Road and then right at the crossing on Mirza Ismail Road. After they passed the city courts where most of the bicycles, cycle-rickshaws and handcarts turned left into Johri bazaar, the traffic thinned. They had to dismount at the entrance to Purana Ghat where the road narrowed and climbed steeply. Hemmed in from both sides by old gardens, garden houses and temples, the road did not reveal the slightest clue to its colourful past at this point, nor later when it wound through the outskirts of Jaipur. It was, in fact, part of an ancient route from the north to the central and eastern parts of the country and of the first great road laid out by the British—a 360-mile stretch from Agra to Deesa. The Agra road had always been vital for trade and the passage of the mighty armies of the Mughal and British empires.

Most of the garden houses, constructed in the nineteenth century and the early part of the twentieth by ministers, high officials of the Jaipur durbar and rich merchants of the city, now lay deserted. The gardens, laid out in the Persian *charbagh* design with fruit trees, flower beds, water courses, fountains and an open central pavilion, were in a state of decay. In the last decade, though, there had been a tentative renewal. The Golcha gardens at the entrance to the Ghat, built by one of the richest families of Jaipur, and the Sitaram temple, constructed by another well-known jeweller, were part of this revival.

By the time they reached the temple, lying next to an elegant row of *chhatris* opposite the Vidiadhar garden, the boys were sweating from the heat and the effort required to push their bicycles up the steep slope. Climbing up a short flight of three steps, they squeezed past a dog sleeping upon its own shadow in front of the gate to enter the temple's large, well-maintained garden with its neat flower beds and a grove of carefully tended mango trees. Standing in the middle of the garden and enclosed by a low marble balustrade, most of the temple was an open pavilion with colonnaded and foliated arches that provided ornate frames for the distant Nahargarh fort squatting on top of a dun-coloured rocky hill. The enclosed inner sanctum, with a marble spire on the top, was at the far left of the pavilion. The door to the sanctum was open but curtained, the curtains drawn back three times a day to give the devotees a glimpse of the temple deities, Rama and his consort Sita, each time with a change of costume. In a far corner to the right of the sanctum, the boys saw a group of about twenty men and five youths of their own age sitting in a semicircle, listening intently to a small man wrapped in coarse white cloth and sitting in a lotus position on the marble floor. Most of the men were in their late thirties or forties, dhoti-clad shopkeepers spending an agreeable afternoon in elevating spiritual pursuits before they headed back to the bazaars to cope with the evening rush of customers. The youths were harder to place, although Vivek recognized one of them, a newcomer to the wrestling gymnasium near Chandpole gate with whom he had not yet grappled. From the way they looked at Baba with a mixture of devotion and proprietorial familiarity, they looked more like disciples than casual visitors

Baba Ram Das stopped talking when he saw the boys approaching and the other men turned their heads to see what had engaged his attention.

'Where do you come from?' Baba asked, smiling a welcome.

'From the city,' Vivek replied for all of them.

'Are you students?'

'Yes. At Maharaja College.'

'You have a fiery light in your eyes,' Baba said, looking directly at Vivek. 'It indicates the noble and generous nature of a lion.'

Then, pointing toward Kamal,' His light is more that of a fox.'

The men laughed.

'Come, sit,' he said gently to Kamal, making up for the sting of his last remark.

Vivek found Baba's presence much less striking than he had expected. Short and slightly plump, Baba had delicately chiselled, almost feminine features. His closely cropped grey beard and darker hair dusted with silver highlighted the youthful sheen of his smooth brown skin.

'As I was saying,' Baba continued his interrupted answer to one of the questioners, 'when merely hearing the name of Rama just once will move you to tears and make your hair stand on end, then you may know for certain that you do not have to perform prayers or other devotions anymore. Only when you reach this state will you have the right to renounce all rituals. Or, rather, the rituals will drop away by themselves. Then it will be enough if you repeat only the name of Rama or even simply Om. But to reach such a state requires an arduous spiritual journey. The requirements of the soul are infinitely harder to meet than the needs of the body.'

Kamal, who would rather have been lying under the shade of a tree in Ramnivas Gardens, shelling peanuts and watching cricket, turned to Vivek with a look that was a mixture of conspiracy and exasperation, the latter accentuated by a brief rolling up of the eyes. He held strong views on the existence of a soul and a life after death, views he loudly avowed in the college canteen during the breaks from classes to provoke other students, most of them highly religious.

'There is no such thing as a soul,' he would declaim. 'You confuse soul with your consciousness. And you find your consciousness so splendid that you cannot bear the thought of it not existing for ever. Well, the bad news is that consciousness ends with the death of the brain. What is left when the brain dies is fast-decaying flesh. And then, after cremation, ash and a few charred bones. Even these disappear when they are thrown into a river. All that remains of a person is homeopathic doses of carbon in the water of the oceans. Sorry, no soul.'

As Baba talked, Kamal's look became imploring. Finally, receiving his friend's nod to go ahead, he called out to Baba, who turned his head to look enquiringly at the boys.

'Baba,' Kamal began politely, 'we hear that you have visions of gods.'

Baba agreed, smiling.

'Modern science has shown there is no such thing as a vision. It is all an illusion of the mind. How do you know that your visions are not mere hallucinations?'

'I don't, since I have never had hallucinations,' Baba replied, the serenity of his smile unchanging. 'But I have heard that a man who hallucinates is afraid that the hallucination will return whereas I cannot wait to have the next vision. And hallucinations ruin a man's constitution. You see mad men with emaciated frames and hollowed cheeks. But visions make one feel healthier, brighter, glowing with well-being. Look how plump I am!'

There was a ripple of uneasy laughter among the men. They had sensed the threat emanating from the students.

Kamal was not one to give up without a struggle.

'Baba, have you seen God?'

'Yes, just as clearly as I see you,' Baba Ram Das said, his smile a shade warmer. 'I have talked to Him more intimately than I am talking to you. But, my son, who wants to see God? People yearn for money and fame. Who yearns for God? They weep copious tears if their loved ones are absent. Who sheds tears for Him?'

'Baba, isn't it true that all these holy men are parasites upon our poor country?' Kamal was now angry, and ignored the warning pressure of Vivek's hand on his arm. 'All a guru does is rob his disciples of their wealth.'

'No, son,' Baba said. 'The guru does not rob the disciples of their money, but of their ignorance. He does not take away their wealth and property but their anxieties and sins. He does not recommend the renunciation of material goods but only makes them renounce bondage.'

There was a murmur of approval from the assembly. As Vivek looked at the rapt faces of the men, he could sense their unconditional love in the way they drank in Baba with their eyes. He was impressed. This man was not crazy. No madman could have inspired so much affection from virtual strangers. He saw Nemi Chand staring at Baba's face with the shining eyes of the fresh devotee and even Suresh seemed to be wavering. Kamal was the only one to hold out. With an expression of distaste on his face, he was looking out of the pavilion at the distant ramparts of Nahargarh and the fortified walls that snaked over the contours of the brown desert hills.

'No more of this talk,' Baba said, clapping his hands, suddenly capricious. 'Let us sing to Lord Rama.'

Then, noticing Vivek beckoning to his friends to get up and leave, he asked: 'Don't you like to sing to the Lord?'

'I am not sure if I am a believer.'

'You don't have to believe to sing. Faith comes with the song. Even if you have not loved the Lord, even if you have turned your back on a life of devotion, to lament these failings in song is to return to Rama's fold. To sing one's sins is to make contact with the Lord.'

Hesitant at first and then with increasing vigour the boys, except for Kamal who remained defiantly silent, joined in the singing of the bhajan. It was a well-known song in which Hanuman replies to Ravana's wife when she seeks to tempt the monkey-god with the offer of delicious fruit from the demon-king's garden so as to make him drop the heavenly weapon he is carrying back to Rama.

Am I in need of fruit?
I have the fruit that makes this life
Fruitful indeed. Within my heart
The tree of Rama grows
Bearing salvation for its fruit.

Under the wish-fulfilling tree
Of Rama do I sit at ease,
Plucking whatever fruit I will.
But if you speak of fruit—
No beggar, I, for common fruit.
Behold, I go,
Leaving a bitter fruit for you.

Even as he joined in the bhajan, clapping to its rhythm but humming almost all the words—for the song was from an era of his childhood tantalizingly beyond the reach of memory, its topography blanketed by a thick fog of forgetfulness—Vivek was observing Baba closely. In the medley of many male voices, Baba's high-pitched alto stood out in the sweetness and the intensity of feeling animating it. His eyes

became more and more abstracted as the song proceeded but
he did not go into a samadhi. At the end of the bhajan, there
was a glitter in Baba's eyes and his face turned pale. His body
shuddered once as if he was feeling giddy. But though the
upper part of his body swayed, he did not fall.

The song continued to reverberate in Vivek's mind for a
while after its last note had faded. Piercing the fog, it lit up a
scene from that bygone era when he was a little boy and his
love affair with his mother was at its height, the time when
her slightest absence was an agony threatening to shatter his
tenuous composure. He heard their intermingled voices from
long ago raised in song during the morning prayer in her puja
room. He could clearly see the small marble idol of Krishna
with his flute, the base of the idol heaped with fresh
marigolds and white narcissi. Once again, he smelt the
cloying perfume of the puja room, distilled from flowery
scents and the fragrance of incense smoke. Oddly enough,
although his mother was a central figure in the tableaux laid
out before his mind's eye, he could not see her clearly. She
was an abiding but diffuse presence, luminous but lacking
definition.

Suddenly Vivek felt the press of a hand on his shoulder.
He looked up into the kindest eyes he had ever seen, a
kindness shot through with skeins of love, like gold thread
shimmering in a length of brocade. Many years later, he read
a journalist's description of Baba's eyes as those of a lover
looking at the beloved in that short span of time after desire
has been sated, when the bodies have separated but the souls
have not. When Baba motioned to him to follow, Vivek did
not hesitate, and walked after him to the inner sanctum of the

temple on the opposite side of the pavilion.

The spell finally broke when Vivek found himself standing in front of the gold-plated idols of Rama and Sita, dimly lit by earthen oil lamps. Baba was holding his hands in both of his own. He pulled Vivek close to him. His voice was agitated when he spoke.

'Where have you been? You have come so late. Why were you so cruel to make me wait all these days?'

Involuntarily, Vivek turned to look over his shoulder. For an instant he thought Baba was talking to someone behind him. To the boy's horror, pressing his hands to his heart, Baba now began to sob as he spoke.

'Oh, how I have longed to pour my spirit into the heart of someone who is fit to receive it. Will you come again soon? Tomorrow? Promise me you will come!'

'The man is mad!' Vivek thought. With some difficulty he pulled his hands free of Baba's convulsive grip.

'Promise you will come soon, and alone,' Baba repeated in childish entreaty.

Unable to evade the piteous look in his eyes, Vivek mumbled a 'yes' and hurried back to where the friends were sitting. Imagine! Talking to a stranger as if to a lover! 'Definitely a screw loose!' was what he later said to his friends when they were pedalling their way home, ignoring Nemi Chand's plaintive 'Tea at Niro's' as they passed the restaurant.

'I imagined he'd look like Moses. Like Charlton Heston in *The Ten Commandments*. Remember? We saw it in the morning show at Prem Prakash? Or at least like Tagore,' Suresh said when they stopped at the Panch Batti roundabout where they would take their separate ways home.

'Those long silvery locks and flowing white beard sported by Tagore always made him look such a phony, like an ancient rishi in the posters they sell in the bazaars,' Kamal said. 'This man is not a phony, just crazy.'

Vivek did not join in his friends' laughter. He could not deny that he had been strongly moved by the man. There was a childlike openness about him, a complete lack of guile which he had never encountered in another adult. Perhaps madmen were equally guileless, yet Ram Das could not be completely mad. Madmen could not love whereas Ram Das seemed so full of love that it was embarrassing. But he was definitely an eccentric, Vivek finally decided.

Chapter Five

Vivek was awakened by a loud grinding of gears and the deep-throated rumble of the engine as their old Vauxhall began to climb up the gorge in which the old capital of Amber was set. With its dilapidated though still resplendent havelis, Amber was like an ancient temple abruptly abandoned by its resident deity.

The climb was short and the locking of gears changed into a high-pitched whine as the Vauxhall began to descend the winding road into the plain below. In the distance, the city walls of Jaipur, which had replaced Amber as the capital 250 years ago, shimmered like a golden mirage in the rays of the setting sun. The land on the right of the road was dotted with temples, havelis and garden houses, most of them hidden behind high stone walls. Towards the left was the Maharaja's hunting reserve, acres of flat, low-lying grassland, teeming with peacocks and herds of black buck but bare of all human habitation except the palatial hunting lodge. During the rainy season much of the reserve came under water, a magnet for flocks of wild geese and the Maharaja's shooting parties.

Dusk was falling when they drove through the northern

city gate into the bazaar. Temple bells had begun to ring for the evening service. Jaipur had more temples—over a thousand—than any other Indian city with the exception of Benares. The bazaar was getting crowded with the evening rush of customers. With their cupolas, towers and scalloped arches, an eclectic mix of Rajput, Mughal and European influences, all the buildings were painted a uniform pink, a striking, unusual shade of pink derived from a mixture of lime and red earth. Many of the buildings in the bazaar had shops on the street level, living quarters on the second story, and viewing galleries at the very top with projecting, latticed windows for the women to watch the ceremonial processions so loved by Jaipur's rulers and its citizens.

There were five people in the car now rattling through the bazaar to the house on Bhagwan Das Road where Trilok Nath waited for his family to arrive. Vivek's grand-uncle, the younger brother of his father's father and the putative head of the family, was sprawled in the front seat of the car, his fat thigh leaving the harried driver little room to shift gears. Vivek's grand-aunt, Sharada Devi, occupied the bulk of the back seat. Her ample girth was squeezing Vivek's mother against the right door and occasionally threatened to squash the slight boy against the left. Every once in a while, Sharada Devi would shift in her seat, contracting the overflowing flesh of her limbs to give Vivek a little more space but resolutely ignoring the boy's mother. Vivek did not like his grand-aunt. Not for anything she had done to him. In fact, she was very fond of the boy. There was a genuine warmth that came through despite the exaggerated gestures of affection and extravagant endearments she used whenever other people—especially Vivek's father—were present. At such times, to his utter embarrassment, she would take him in her arms, nuzzle his hair and coo endearments in a babyish voice. If his mother also happened to be around, Sharada Devi would almost always reproach her: 'Maheshwari, look how thin the boy has become! You don't feed him enough. I will have to take on the responsibility of looking after him—and in my old age! Ah, you young women . . . ,' she would say, sighing and shaking her head.

Vivek disliked his grand-aunt for the way she treated his mother when his father was away at work. She was invariably rude and sarcastic in her comments about Maheshwari's running of the household. She made impossible demands on her cooking skills and then held forth on her shortcomings. Maheshwari bore the daily humiliations in silence. At the very beginning of their marriage, when she had complained to her husband about his aunt's behaviour, Trilok Nath had made it abundantly clear that he felt beholden to his aunt even more than to the mother who had given birth to him. Sharada Devi had brought him up when his father left home to become a sadhu and his mother, in her baffled grief, withdrew completely from the business of running a household and raising a five-year-old son, spending most of her days closeted in the prayer room. His debt to his aunt was so great, Trilok Nath bluntly told his bride, that he expected her to adjust to Sharada Devi's ways and not give the old lady any cause for complaint. Even before she became Trilok Nath's bride, Maheshwari, like most girls from orthodox households, had half-expected and half-feared that she would have to play the role of the suffering daughter-in-law for which tradition and her own mother had amply prepared her. She could thus bear her tribulations with a minimum of tears, keeping her tattered dignity intact with the silent support of Vivek's grand-uncle and the ardent partisanship of her son who made it evident to the amused adults that he loved his mother above all else in the world and that he would defend her with all the might of his passionate little heart.

Above all, Maheshwari had the consolations of a deep faith, that grew stronger with the years, in a benign God, however inscrutable His ways. There was not one prescribed fast she did not keep, nor one ritual she ignored or forgot during her increasingly long sojourns in the prayer room which she had taken over after the death of Vivek's grandmother. This room became her refuge. Vivek was his mother's enthusiastic helper in the trappings of her religious life. He brought her the flowers, freshly plucked every morning by the gardener, for her morning puja. He sat next to her—legs crossed, palms folded, eyes closed, imitating her devotion as she prayed to the white marble idol of Krishna that she had inherited from her mother-in-law. He tried to imitate the cadences of her *Ramayana*-reading voice when he repeated the verses from the epic after her. He insisted on accompanying her to every place in the neighbourhood where a chanting of the *Ramayana* by professional singers was to take place, staying awake till the end of the performance, however far it went into the night. If a sadhu came to the house for alms, Vivek would enthusiastically rush to the kitchen to bring the mendicant rotis and vegetables and coins from his mother's purse while she engaged the holy man in talk of spiritual matters.

Vivek worshipped his mother, literally. In the morning, after his father left for office, Maheshwari began her prayers with the washing of the stone feet of Lord Krishna's idol and then drinking some of this water. Vivek would take a sip of the water too, but then insist that his mother dip her big toe in another cup of water. He would then drink from the cup, delighting in the play of embarrassment and joy on Maheshwari's face.

Sharada Devi grumbled to the servants and to her husband, made caustic remarks about Maheshwari's piety which she warned would bankrupt the household one day, but was wary of an open confrontation where she might have to take a firm stand against the many irritating demonstrations of Maheshwari's faith. Religious life, even of a lowly daughter-in-law, was sacrosanct. It could be interfered with only if the woman was grossly neglectful of her family, which Maheshwari was not. Sharada Devi was especially careful not to protest too loudly against Maheshwari's largesse to the sadhus. Most of them, everyone knew, were shirkers, beggars in disguise. But she had to keep these thoughts to herself since her own brother-in-law, Trilok Nath's father, had left home to lead a sadhu's wandering life. All Sharada Devi could do was to remonstrate with Maheshwari on the amount of time Vivek spent in the prayer room and point out, often and loudly, that in imitating his mother's frequent fasts the boy was not eating enough. Then, one day, Sharada Devi at last got her chance.

It was one of those cold January days for which Delhi in

its collective amnesia induced by the long hot summers is always ill prepared. The fog had lingered beyond noon before a weak wintry sun finally succeeded in dissipating its last tendrils. It was late in the afternoon. Vivek's mother and grand-aunt were huddled under thick quilts in their rooms for the afternoon nap. Vivek was standing outside on the lawn, watching the gardener plant rose cuttings and dahlias for the spring, when the sadhu appeared at the gate.

'Give in the name of God,' the sadhu called out, his powerful voice accustomed to giving commands so different from the wheedling whine of the ordinary beggar.

Vivek walked up to him. The sadhu was tall, well-built and lushly-bearded, his half-naked presence as authoritative as his deep voice.

'My mother is sleeping,' the five-year-old said, bringing his palms together and raising them to his bowed head exactly as he had seen his mother greet other holy men.

'Then *you* shall earn the merit of giving today,' the sadhu said, smiling down at the boy. 'It is cold. You can bring me a shawl.'

Vivek did not hesitate. He ran back to the house, and instead of a shawl he brought for the sadhu his father's new woollen suit, the one with the closed collar that government officials had begun to wear since Independence. Stitched by Kirpa Ram Tailors of Connaught Place less than a month back, the dove-grey flannel suit was his father's favourite.

'Bless you!' the sadhu said running his fingers over the soft material of a suit he would never wear.

'Remember, boy, always give away what you love the most if the gift is to have merit or meaning. One day, when you are older, you will understand.' The sadhu did not look back as he walked away with a firm stride toward the nearby Lodi Gardens.

When Vivek's father returned from work in the evening to find his almirah open and his favourite suit missing, he was furious. Terrified of his father's anger, Vivek confessed, half hoping that he would be forgiven, for he hadn't really stolen it. But his confession only made his father angrier.

'It's not the boy's fault,' Sharada Devi said, trying to deflect rather than placate Trilok Nath's anger. Maheshwari stood haplessly in one corner of the room, her eyes focussed on an invisible spot near her feet while Trilok Nath's rage swirled and surged around her. Vivek was not frightened for his mother. He knew that his father could never sustain his anger for more than a few minutes.

'You can pray and fast all you want but spare the boy,' Trilok Nath said to his wife after he had calmed down. 'He is not a woman. All the good karma he needs, he will earn himself through his manly deeds.'

'You don't have to lock him up whenever a sadhu appears at the gate but we must be very careful,' Sharada Devi said, her voice dripping with sweet reasonableness. 'Remember? His horoscope?' And then the three of them exchanged that special look of complicity which excludes children from adult secrets, even when the adults are less than intimate. Years later, when they were living in Jaipur and Vivek was in his first year of college, he learned from his mother that the secret had to do with his grandfather.

Durga Prasad had been a promising young lawyer in Delhi, although some thought he was too timid to rise to the top of a profession that required brashness, when, suddenly, at the age of twenty-five and a few days after the birth of his son Trilok, he decided to renounce the world and become a wandering monk. His family and friends were shocked by the decision, about which they found out only after Durga Prasad had disappeared from Delhi. Granted, there were some family problems which could have weighed heavily on his sensitive, perhaps even over-sensitive, nature. His widowed mother had taken to her bed in silent hopelessness after a beloved nephew cheated her of all her gold ornaments. His younger brother, Kali Prasad, who had not shown any inclination for paid work, preferring instead to spend his time playing cards with his other unemployed friends, had not become more responsible after marriage as Durga Prasad had hoped. Moreover, Kali Prasad's spirited young wife, Sharada Devi, in defiance of a time-honoured familial hierarchy, had begun to lord it over her elder sister-in-law. Durga Prasad, people said later, was fed up, especially with the women's constant bickering and his wife's nagging demand that he exercise his authority to restore the natural order of domination and deference between the two warring women. But such problems were not unusual. Everyone knew that nothing else in this world compared with the feelings of peace and security that resulted from a harmonious joint family and that nothing also matched the pain and suffering that resulted when this harmony was out of joint. But wise people knew that both the harmony and its disruption were short-lived, following each other like day and night, and they did not let their equanimity be affected by this natural ebb and flow of family life.

Whatever his reasons, Durga Prasad left his Daryaganj home for the Tis Hazari courts one morning, wearing his lawyer's black coat and tie and carrying his black leather briefcase bulging with case files, and never came back. He left behind a letter for his brother, informing him about his decision to become a sadhu and committing his wife, son and their mother to his care. For the next twelve years, the family remained ignorant about his whereabouts. There were rumours, of course. He was variously reported to have been spotted in Benares, Rishikesh, Hardwar and even in the southern temple town of Madurai, wearing saffron or white robes, head shaved or with matted locks, face bearded or clean-shaven.

The family was concerned but fortunately there were no immediate financial worries since there was enough money for them to live in modest comfort for some years. Kali Prasad may have been indolent but he was a good-natured young man, without any major vices such as gambling or a fondness for the prostitutes of G.B. Road which, everyone agreed, could quickly lead to a family's ruin. He wisely left his nephew's upbringing, the running of the household—Durga Prasad's wife having retired to the puja room after her husband's disappearance—and the management of the family's finances in Sharada Devi's capable hands (for many years the young woman ran a small but profitable moneylending venture) and began to lead the kind of life to which he had always aspired. This was the life of a man who was neither cursed with talent nor damned by ambition and was fortunate enough not to have to work for a living. He filled his days with easy luxuries and small pleasures: wrestling with friends on the banks of the Jamuna followed by oil massages in the morning; gossiping and playing cards with friends in the afternoon; strolling through Chandni Chowk in the evening, eating *chaat* and ogling pretty women; and at night, after dinner, playing gramaphone records of Mallika Pukhraj and Master Madan. He loved children and although he never had any of his own, he regarded his nephew as his son and spent any free time he had at home playing with the child.

In accordance with the hoary custom that a sadhu revisit his native place twelve years after leaving it, Durga Prasad returned to Delhi a few days after Trilok Nath's twelfth birthday. He did not come home, though, preferring instead to stay in a rest house for wandering sadhus which was attached to a Shiva temple near the Purana Qila. Here he was spotted by one of his distant cousins who was a regular devotee at this temple. The cousin informed Kali Prasad about his brother's presence in the city and said that he looked weak, perhaps ill. With the help of two friends, Kali Prasad forcibly brought his brother back home and locked him up in his old room when he tried to run away. Durga Prasad's protest against his confinement took the form of a refusal to eat. After initially answering his wife's entreaty to resume his life as a householder with a muttered 'What are you to me, woman?' Durga Prasad rebuffed any further attempt at conversation by maintaining a stubborn silence. Alarmed at his brother's deteriorating health, Kali Prasad had no choice but to let him go.

The next time a member of the family saw him was after five years. Durga Prasad's wife, accompanied by two other

widowed cousins, had at last fulfilled a long-cherished wish
to go to Benares for a pilgrimage. One day, as the three
women were walking down an alley leading to the
Vishwakarma ghat, Durga Prasad's wife slipped and fell
down. A sadhu who was passing by pulled her up by the
hair—since a sadhu cannot touch a woman's body—and as
she stood up, she came face to face with her husband. As
soon as he recognized her, Durga Prasad let go of her hair
and ran away. His wife brushed down the soiled folds of her
saree and continued on her pious rounds without looking
back at her fleeing husband.

'A few weeks before your birth,' Vivek's mother said, 'we
heard from the priest of the Shiva temple where your
grandfather stayed the last time he was in Delhi that he had
died in Benares. When you were a few months old, your aunt
was the first to remark on your strong resemblance to your
grandfather. Then at your naming ceremony, some of the old
relatives who had known your grandfather since he was a
boy said that you were his spitting image—with the same
large, slightly bulging eyes and long Buddha-like ears. Some
even speculated whether your grandfather's soul had become
reincarnated in your body—a speculation your father was
swift to discourage. And then we got your horoscope made.
The horoscope predicted that before the age of thirty you too
would leave the world and become a sadhu.

'"Fate only means an increased probability," your father
said when he saw the horoscope before he locked it away.
"Human effort can decrease this probability till it is no
longer fateful. No son of mine will ever become a wandering
monk. We have enough of them in this benighted land."'

It was not till Trilok Nath came to Jaipur with his family two years after the princely states of Rajputana were integrated into a newly independent India, when Vivek was six years old, that he took charge of his son's education and began his campaign to defeat the future foretold for his son in the horoscope. Vivek's early childhood, pervaded by his mother's gentle presence and that of her benevolent gods and goddesses, now came to an abrupt end. His mother accepted his desertion as she had Sharada Devi's slights and her husband's indifference—with stoic calm. It was in the order of things that after a certain age a mother surrender the son to the father and the world of men he represented. She still fed and clothed her son's body with love, but accepted that henceforth his mind would be poured into a mould crafted by his father. Perhaps later, after he became a man, she could try to build him a bridge back to their former two-person universe. 'Do you remember, when you were a little boy . . .?' she would begin with an appeal to his memory, uncertain all the while if he would accept her offer. She wished she had had a daughter. Daughters were different.

There was nothing orthodox—at least as far as religion was concerned—or other-worldly about Trilok Nath. He called himself an agnostic, which meant that he did not give much thought to the rewards and tribulations of an afterlife, involved as he was in fully savouring the pleasures of the present one.

'The only purpose of life is the propagation of the

species. All the rest is priestly mumbo-jumbo,' he would say. 'The aims of life are simple: earn money, marry, have children, lead a happy life yourself and contribute to the happiness of others as far as it is in your power to do so.'

A stocky man with an infectious laugh, he loved to give parties which were marked by an abundance of good food (specially prepared by a Muslim cook hired for the occasion), intelligent conversation, and some heavy-handed flirting with the wives of his colleagues—looking deep into their eyes while singing soulful ghazals. Trilok Nath was especially fond of highly seasoned chicken and lamb curries which his wife and aunt, being vegetarians, had the cook prepare for him separately in one corner of the kitchen. And his first step in his son's education was to wean him away from his vegetarianism and awaken his taste buds to the pleasures of eating meat.

'All vegetarians are placid creatures, without spirit, easily subdued. Why do you think the British ruled us for hundreds of years? Not because of superior arms but because of their independent, fighting spirit which comes from eating beef and other meats. An elephant is immensely strong but easily enslaved by man. A cat may be small but will always struggle to preserve its independence.'

He enrolled Vivek in the Jesuit-run St Xavier's School, opposite their house on Bhagwan Das Road. He helped him with his homework and encouraged his participation in school sports. After Vivek, who was athletically gifted, began his steady climb through the school's junior hockey and cricket teams to captain the senior squads, Trilok Nath turned up for all his son's matches played on Sunday mornings when he did not have to go to his office.

Throughout his ten years at St Xaviers, Vivek was a very good student. He excelled at history and English but had an inexplicable aversion to mathematics which prevented him from taking the top position in his class. Trilok Nath was understanding, even proud of his son's deficiency.

'Mathematics,' he would say, 'is a grocer's craft.'

On Vivek's twelfth birthday, his father gave him the key to the glass cupboard in his room where he kept his small library of books.

'One day you will be able to read most of them,' he said.

The books were in English, Urdu and Persian, languages Trilok Nath knew well. He was especially fond of history and could recite, to his son's awe and delight, long passages from Gibbon's *Fall of the Roman Empire* which occupied the pride of place in the middle of the top shelf. He loved the poems of Hafiz and the sonnets of Shakespeare. But his collection was singularly devoid of religious books, except the Bible, since he considered the teachings of Jesus of Nazareth to be the acme of spiritual thought with which every educated person should be acquainted, without necessarily agreeing with its contents.

'There is nothing you can learn from our ancient sages or our *shastras*,' he would say to his son. 'They are the source of Hindu weakness and the superstition rampant in our land.'

Every afternoon around five when he returned from office, he took Vivek along with him to Jaipur Club. There he played a couple of sets of vigorous tennis while Vivek swam in the swimming pool or, when he was older, played tennis with the sons of his father's colleagues. After a shower and a change of clothes, father and son sat companionably around a table on the club lawns, sipping ice-cold lemonade while waiters in white coats scurried softly around them, switching on the garden lamps to keep the swiftly advancing desert darkness at bay.

Vivek enjoyed being his father's son even when he was older, though he was sometimes embarrassed by his father's public demonstrations of pride and affection. Trilok Nath encouraged his son to participate in his own work life whenever circumstances permitted such participation, thus giving the son access to what is perhaps the most valuable part of a father's life. Vivek's memory of the very first time his father took him along to a public function, a few months after they arrived in Jaipur, always remained vivid, presenting itself in ever new hues rather than fading away with the passage of time.

It was the day of the Dashera celebration in the City Palace which Trilok Nath, as the newly appointed secretary to the Rajpramukh, the Maharaja of Jaipur, was expected to attend, even though the celebration properly belonged to the old feudal order that was fated to disappear in Independent India's republic dispensation. Dressed in a cream-coloured raw silk kurta-and-pyjama outfit that his father had recently got stitched for him, six-year-old Vivek had looked surprisingly grown up. Maheshwari, watching her son from the veranda with a mixture of pride and wistfulness, waved as the car drove away but Vivek, who was animatedly chattering away to his father, did not look back. In the palace, where the state of Rajasthan had come into existence in a glittering ceremony on 30 March 1949, Trilok Nath introduced his son to his new boss. The dashing Maharaja, resplendent in his magenta silk turban, a riot of ruby and emerald necklaces spilling over his crimson and gold brocaded *achkan,* had smiled at the boy and ruffled his hair. Watched by the ladies of the court from behind windows of latticed stone, the Maharaja had then begun his ceremonial worship of arms and weapons of war. Afterwards, they had watched the Dashera procession, led by the Jaipur state troops, cavalry and camel riders, accompanied by military bands and followed by the Maharaja's personal bodyguard riding their matched black horses, file out of the palace gates. The Maharaja's own golden carriage, drawn by six white horses, was followed by all of Jaipur's nobility: smartly dressed, bejewelled and mustachioed men riding grandly caparisoned horses. Soon, shouts of 'Maharaja Man Singh *ki jai*' from people who were crowding the streets and every window and balcony along the royal route, came in like the muffled crash of waves breaking against the high walls of the palace.

Vivek felt his father's arm tightening around his shoulders. 'One day,' his father said, in the grip of some strong, sweet emotion, 'one day . . .' The love and pride in his voice, more than the unfinished sentence, seemed to promise Vivek a glorious future.

In 1954 Trilok Nath was appointed the district magistrate of Jaipur, and in the following three years Vivek often accompanied him on official tours during his school vacations. These tours, some lasting for a week, were virtual expeditions. Camels loaded with tents, camping equipment and food stuff, set off early in the morning while father and son followed at a more leisurely pace with a retinue of servants, policemen and court clerks. By the evening they would reach the village that was their destination. Tents would be set up and cooking fires lighted. Trilok Nath would inspect the revenue records, hear complaints and adjudicate disputes. A stream of favour-seekers from the village would call on him. Drawing on a collective memory of subjugation reaching back hundreds of years, the villagers were well-versed in the arts of flattery. Making complimentary remarks about the District Magistrate sahib's son and indulging the child's every whim was a part of their practised repertoire. Just nine or ten years old, Vivek was still unaware that the fawning he received from others in his father's retinue or from the villagers was not to be confused with love, and that he was not the centre of everyone else's universe as he was of his family's.

At Maharaja College, which he joined at the age of seventeen after finishing school, Vivek soon acquired a reputation for unconventional brilliance. Enrolled for a degree in philosophy, he read widely, although unsystematically, in popular science, history and psychology. He had inherited his father's gift for easily committing to memory many pages of a book he had read only once, and would astonish his classmates with long quotes from Herbert Spencer, Bertrand Russell, Marx and Jung, much to the silent suffering of his teachers. His prodigious memory, however, seemed to desert him at the time of the annual examinations, which he passed in a modest second division. Given his plans for his son, the examination results had begun to cause Vivek's father some concern. All in all, though, Trilok Nath was proud of his son and revelled in the praise of his colleagues who thought Vivek was 'a born leader of men'.

With his thick, wavy black hair, large and luminous though slightly bulging eyes, and muscular body, Vivek was a handsome boy who was both unaware of and uninterested in the effect he had on the opposite sex. This further increased his mystique for some of the more intellectual students who looked up to him as a model to emulate in their own struggles against the sexual obsessions of youth. Whether or not his chastity came naturally to him, it was certainly strengthened by the ethos of wrestling. To the delight of Kali Prasad who was reminded of his own youthful days on the banks of the Jamuna and with the approval of Trilok Nath who considered wrestling to be the manliest of Indian sports, Vivek had become a passionate wrestler. Each morning he woke up at dawn and ran the three miles to the wrestling gymnasium near Chandpole Gate to build stamina. The gymnasium was run by a professional wrestler who in the olden days had won many laurels for the Jaipur durbar in competitive bouts against wrestlers from other princely states and had marched on ceremonial occasions in royal processions through the bazaars of the capital.

Vivek's training regimen was strict and his standards high. After a hurried bath, he would don the wrestler's habit, the loincloth, and then together with a dozen other young men from different social classes and professions, none of them a student, he would get down to preparing the ten-yard square wrestling pit from fresh mud and straw. This was followed by an hour of various kinds of weight training, deep knee bends and jack-knifing push ups. The teacher would then pair him off with another budding wrestler to grapple and practice moves and countermoves. After an hour of this exhausting trial of strength, it was heavenly to roll in the earth of the wrestling pit and partake of the mud's cooling and reinvigorating qualities. On returning home after another bath at the gymnasium, he normally found Trilok Nath already seated at the dining table for his English-style breakfast of porridge with milk, buttered toast and omelette, the last Indianized by the addition of chopped onions and green chillies. Vivek's breakfast, though, lovingly prepared by his mother, was what all wrestlers normally ate in the morning: a litre of fresh, frothing milk, a small slab of home-made ghee and a quantity of shelled almonds left to soak overnight in water.

Vivek had learnt from his teacher that of the many virtues wrestling demanded from its practitioners, such as simplicity, honesty, cleanliness, none was higher than celibacy. Semen was the locus of the wrestler's strength and character. Milk, ghee and almonds, the primary ingredients of the wrestler's diet, built up a store of high energy semen which was vital for the enhancement of bodily strength. According to his teacher, wrestling was not only a physical activity but the meeting point of muscles and morals, and Vivek loved being a part of its dedicated world. The small group of students who began to gather around him in his third year of college not only admired his intellectual brilliance but were also in awe of his physical prowess and determination. He seemed destined to prosperity and fame. They could never have imagined the changes that his father's sudden death was to bring about in Vivek, dramatically altering the course of his life.

Ram Das

The road of excess leads to the palace
of wisdom.

—WILLIAM BLAKE,
The Marriage of Heaven and Hell

Chapter Six

Amba was worried. Perhaps she should not have forced the boy to go out that afternoon. On his return, Gopal had sat listlessly in one corner of the hut, his sight glued to the space in front of his feet. He refused to answer her questions on where he had been, burying his head in his knees when she persisted. In spite of her coaxing, he did not eat dinner and went hungry to bed.

Around three in the morning, Amba was awakened by a loud scream. Gopal was on his knees, the knuckles of his right hand pressing into a spot at the base of the spine just inside the cleft of his buttocks. His eyes were pinched tightly shut as waves of pain flitted across his face. Her first thought was that a scorpion had bitten him. She quickly lit the kerosene lantern and pushing the boy to one side, turned his mat over. There was no sign of the scorpion. Raising the lantern, she carefully examined the rest of the floor. The scorpion had disappeared. To her relief, Gopal already seemed better. The pain was subsiding as quickly as it had flared up. Soon he fell into a sleep so deep that it seemed to hover near unconsciousness. His body was rigid, without even the occasional twitches that testify to the continuing flow of life while the outer senses lie dormant. Amba sat by his side, waiting for the dawn, often feeling his forehead with her palm to see if he was feverish.

Gopal's eyes were dull when he awoke late in the morning, a slow, bleak awakening from a comatose state. He neither reacted to his mother's voice when she called out to him nor responded to her anxious touch. Around noon, his apathy was replaced by fits of agitation and bizarre behaviour. He would begin to scream and then suddenly stop and start singing snatches of religious songs interspersed with what appeared to be incoherent babbling. Frequently, his limbs stiffened and his eyes glazed over as if there was no one at home in the body.

The vaid came in the afternoon. This time he took the boy's condition more seriously than he had the trances. The nerves that carry the mind to the sensory and motor organs are dry, was his considered diagnosis. The mind's connection to these organs was seriously weakened. Free of the mind's control, the senses had become uninhibited. He left behind a vial of yellowish liquid to be used as a nasal purge and a bottle of herbal medicine which would remove the dryness of the nerves and strengthen them so that Gopal's mind could once again inform and pervade the senses.

Over the next two days there were some changes but no improvement in Gopal's condition. A couple of hours after the administration of the nasal purge which induced violent fits of sneezing, Gopal's face swelled up to the size of a small melon. As the swelling gradually subsided, his eyes, emerging from the slits into which they had almost disappeared, held an expression even his mother could not recognize as belonging to her son. It was no longer one of withdrawal but of a different kind of absence, as if Gopal was peering into unfamiliar spaces and seeing things hidden from the others. On the fifth day, the doctor from Jaipur arrived on his scheduled monthly visit to Deogarh. After a perfunctory examination during which he pulled up Gopal's eyelids and looked closely at the whites of his eyes, he declared that the boy was suffering from hysteria. The illness had nothing to do with the scorpion bite the boy might or might not have received. He gave the boy an injection and left some white tablets to be taken with milk every twelve hours.

The doctor's medication proved even less effective than the vaid's ministrations. In addition to his earlier symptoms, Gopal now developed some new ones: uncontrollable weeping interspersed with bouts of hysterical laughter. The village astrologer, who had learnt his craft from Gopal's father, was called in. His conclusion was that the boy had become possessed by a particularly vile and stubborn ghost when he was returning from the temple on the evening the illness set in.

'The Balaji temple at Mehndipur is the best place for someone in this condition,' he informed Amba. 'Even the strongest of spirits, those of Muslims grandees, cannot withstand the combined energy of the temple's gods, especially of Lord Hanuman who is the scourge of all malignant spirits.'

Amba was reluctant at first. Exorcism of spirits conjured up images of terrifying men with bloodshot eyes and a manner more wild than that of their possessed patients. It meant a long knife chopping off a chicken's neck and the spraying of hot blood on the possessed patient who swayed before the exorcist in a trance. It meant the possessed person being hit and whipped even as he screamed in pain, while the exorcist shouted even louder as he ordered the spirit to leave.

'There are no exorcists in the Balaji temple,' the astrologer gently reassured her. 'Hanumanji does not need their help. People go to Balaji only after the exorcists have failed. Of course, for the best results you should wait till you receive a personal summons from the god.'

'How is one called?' Amba asked.

'Well, the god usually talks to the possessed person or a close relative directly in a dream,' he explained.

The very next night Amba dreamt of a monkey which was calmly riding a horse through the Rajput quarter. The astrologer agreed that this could indeed be interpreted as an invitation from the monkey-god.

Thus encouraged and with the help of her community which deputed one of its men to accompany mother and son as far as Jaipur where they would change the bus for Mehndipur, Amba decided to make the healing pilgrimage to Balaji.

Under the influence of a strong herbal sedative that the village vaid had insisted the boy drink before mother and son left Deogarh, Gopal dozed most of the time on the long and bumpy bus ride. Gently wiping away the spit that drooled out of a corner of his mouth, and periodically adjusting his head so that it rested on her shoulder and did not slide down her arm with the constant jolting, Amba was filled with tenderness and worry for her odd son. She wondered if she

should have insisted that he go out and play with the other
boys while he was growing up. She wondered if she should
not have firmly discouraged the signs of his precocious
religiosity the very first time they appeared. But she had been
lonely, glad of his company in her daily puja and his help in
the household. She had been proud of a son who was so often
invited to village homes for religious festivals and received by
the families with a mixture of familiarity with which a small
boy is treated and the reverence that is due to a holy man who
sometimes dwells in God. She had often preened inwardly
when the head of a family took her son by the hand or, when
he was smaller, carried him in his arms to seat him at the
front of the assembly, near the priest.

'O Balaji!' Amba silently vowed, 'make him well and I
promise I shall come to your temple every year at the time of
your festival and keep a three-day fast.'

The bus clattered past miles and miles of barren land
dotted with a dusty olive-green scrub and scarred by
dried-out gullies and narrow ravines that stretched out on
either side of the road. Then squat hills, with thorny bushes
and eroded topsoil that exposed the underlying rock, became
frequent. The temple lay at the bottom of one such hill,
hugging its side, four miles off the main road from the bus
stop. After a twenty-minute tonga ride through the
sun-drugged silence of the afternoon, broken only by the
sound of the horse's hooves rhythmically striking against the
metalled road, the sudden din on reaching the lane that led
up to the temple came as a shock. Flat-roofed and without
the lofty spire which distinguishes the great Hindu temples,
the Balaji temple was a simple two-storied structure at the

end of the lane which was lined on both sides by shops and a number of *dharamshalas* erected by the pious for lodging pilgrims.

The temple was distinguished from its neighbours only by its façade which was painted a bilious green. In spite of its fluted columns, small arched windows and stone latticed windows, the building still managed to convey a general impression of shabbiness. Patches of green paint were peeling off the underlying stucco. The space in front of the steps leading into the temple as also the steps themselves were littered with banana skins, crushed marigolds and other assorted refuse. The sides of the temple were crowded by eating places, small provision stores and hawkers selling vegetables and fruit along with gaudy posters and painted clay images of the temple deities, prayer books in various sizes, and other holy bric-a-brac. The shop on the right side of the temple displayed the signboard of a western-style medical practitioner. The good doctor, a stout unshaven man with a roll of fat bulging out between the end of his undervest and the string of his pyjamas, was reclining on a cot, thoughtfully paring his nails as he waited for customers who might have cause to be disappointed with the healing powers of the gods inside the temple. In Balaji, medicine existed as a poor relation to religion, obsequious and faintly disreputable.

Blessed with the eyes of faith, Amba was oblivious to the shabbiness of the temple's surroundings or its unimpressive architecture. What she beheld was not a building of brick and stone but the mansion of benevolent gods who would heal her child. After finding a room in one of the dharamshalas, she spread the bedding she had brought with her on the floor and sat next to Gopal till he fell asleep. She knew he would sleep a while, and decided to walk around in the temple and get some inkling of what awaited her son the following morning. Before she left, she asked her neighbour, a woman who had come to Balaji with her daughter who she believed was possessed, to watch over Gopal.

Climbing up the temple steps to enter the outer courtyard, she was greeted by an unfamiliar aroma, a sweet, smoky smell coming from the direction of the main hall. The courtyard was crowded, mostly by young women, many of them sitting or lying on the floor in oddly contorted postures. Her attention was held by a young girl, seventeen or eighteen years old and quite attractive despite the unnatural pallor of her face. Her loose hair was spread around her head which was jerking from side to side as expressions of pain flitted across her face. Her lips moved in an inaudible murmur, interspersed by full-throated shouts of 'Baba, Baba, I won't go, I won't go!'—the ghost, a male spirit to judge by the timbre of the voice and the gender of the verbs, expressing his refusal to vacate her body. Another girl, barely into her teens, was standing on her head against a wall. Even as Amba stared at the girl, she heard a swishing movement behind her and a shoulder brushed against the back of her legs. She turned to see a girl bounding away in high, leaping somersaults, the acrobatic somersaults taking her from one end of the courtyard to another and back again. Amba looked around but no one else seemed to be noticing the girl, and her gaze slid off incurious eyes.

From the outer courtyard she stepped into the main hall.

On the left side, beyond the columns of the temple, there was
a narrow, dark corridor from where she had a good view of
what was happening in the main hall. As her eyes got
accustomed to the darkness she noticed that she was not
alone. An old woman was squatting next to her, surrounded
by the paraphernalia for ritual worship. There were two
copper pots in front of her, both of them filled with water.
She was counting beads from a rosary in her lap and with
every count she dipped a spoon into one of the pots, took out
a spoonful of water and poured it into the second pot.
Another old woman, with a dark-complexioned face that
almost merged into the surrounding darkness, was standing
next to her. Amba was startled to see an unusually long and
purple tongue protruding out of her mouth. She has become
Mother Kali, Amba said to herself and reflexively bowed in
her direction. The woman raised a withered hand in
benediction and Amba could have sworn that the woman
had pushed her tongue out a little more for her benefit.
Feeling uneasy, she quickly moved back into the main hall
and stepped into the path of a dog who swerved to avoid her.
The dog was hurrying toward the front of the hall, to the
dense crowd pressing against an iron grill behind which lay
the   food   offerings—rice,   grain,   sugar   crystals,
coconut—heaped into a mound. Handfuls of the offerings
were being burnt by a priest in a large brass lamp, producing
sacred ash and the thick smoke that Amba had smelt in the
outer courtyard. Through the smoke and the squares of the
iron grill and over the heads of people pushing and shoving
to get nearer, she saw the idol of Balaji. It was a triangular
piece of stone, vaguely reminiscent of a human head, painted

in ochre and silver colours and with two large black eyes drawn on it to give it the appearance of a face.

She should be getting back soon, Amba thought. The boy may be awake by now. But she also wanted to find out for herself what awaited her son during the next few days, whether the temple was indeed free of fierce exorcists and their painful ministrations as the astrologer had promised. Although exhausted from the bus journey, she still made the effort to climb up to the second floor, to the court of Pret-raja, the king of spirits, a subordinate deity to Balaji yet in many ways more intimately involved in the affairs of ghosts. Here, most people were sitting in an orderly fashion, their prayer books open in front of them, singing hymns in praise of Pret-raja's miracles. The singing was led by a boy of fifteen under the approving eyes of a priest sitting in front of Pret-raja's stone representation enclosed in a protective grill. Pret-raja's idol was as minimalistic as Balaji's. It was painted with the same ochre and silver colours as the image of Balaji and had the same large eyes. The singing was full of devotional excitement although Amba noted with maternal pride that the boy was no match for her son, his voice a little muddy stream compared to the pure and majestic Ganga of Gopal's songs. The singing was punctuated by dull thuds produced by possessed patients who were hitting their backs rhythmically against the walls. Amba went up to the back of the hall which had three iron gates similar to those that bar prison cells. She leant against one of the gates and noticed that the space in front of the other two was already occupied by two girls whose legs were chained to the iron bars. One of the girls began to rattle her chains loudly and occasionally shout in a hoarse voice, 'Stop it! Shut up and stop this nonsense or I'll reduce you all to ashes!'

Some people in the front who heard the girl turned their heads but hurriedly looked away as she grimaced at them and made obscene gestures. She then called her husband, a young man who was desperately trying to ignore her and concentrate on singing the hymns. She loudly asked him to have intercourse with her right away and then attempted to lift up her skirt. This produced the desired result and the husband rushed to her side to stop her. As if she had been waiting for this, the girl caught hold of his arm and sank her teeth into his forearm. He yelled and gave her a hard slap that sent her sprawling against the gate.

'I am fed up,' the man shouted, addressing no one in particular. 'I don't know what happens to her. Rot here for all I care! Show everyone your shameless dramas, I'm going home.' The girl, recovered from the blow, was sitting up and laughing delightedly.

Deeply shocked, Amba hurried down the steps and out of the temple into the busy lane where people from the dharamshalas were milling around the shops and the hawkers, buying vegetables and other ingredients for the evening meal. Since the patients needed to be in a state of purity before an appeal to the gods could have a chance to be successful, spices, onions, garlic and other impure foods were unavailable in the market.

On her return to the boarding house, Amba was relieved to learn from the neighbour that Gopal had slept all through the afternoon and had only just woken up. The neighbour insisted that Amba should not cook on her very first evening at Balaji's and that both mother and son should share the evening meal with her own family.

The evening was pleasantly cool and sitting around the cooking fire in the courtyard in front of their room, eating a simple hot meal, Amba felt the unmistakable stirring of hope. Gopal, too, seemed better. Though still seemingly abstracted, the resident of a different world altogether, he ate his food with an evident though private enjoyment. Small groups were gathered around other cooking fires where people exchanged news on the progress made by their possessed relative or friend during the day's rituals in the temple. There was an occasional scream, a sudden eruption of insane laughter or a loud string of obscenities, but this intrusion of the spirit world was taken calmly in stride. One or two members of the group would get up to soothe the possessed patient while the others carried on with their conversation after a polite pause to acknowledge the ghost who had joined them for a while.

Over the next few days, Gopal's old symptoms disappeared. The frequent periods of agitation that he had suffered during his last days at home gave way to a profound lassitude. His responses were no longer automatic but had to be solicited. The vacant look on his face was not that of an idiot but of someone whose eyes are fated to remain untenanted.

'Her ghost came again today,' the neighbour said, nodding towards her daughter. Amba looked more closely at the dark, thin girl, no more than sixteen years old, who was making the rotis with a quiet efficiency that belied her distressed state.

'What happened to her?' she asked.

'It was very strange,' the mother said. 'One afternoon, a day before she was engaged to get married, Sheela went to the outhouse to urinate and called me to help her with her underwear since she had freshly dyed her hands with henna. On the same night, after we had all gone to bed, we heard her frightened screams. She told us that as she was falling asleep she saw a laughing woman come up and begin to dance on her head, giving her a violent headache. I saw she was badly frightened and tried to calm her as best as I could. For the next two years the dancing woman came again and again, frightening the girl and giving her the same headache. All the exorcists we consulted were of the same opinion, Sheela was possessed by a female ghost. But in spite of their efforts they could not rid Sheela of the spirit's visitations and so we had to bring her to Balaji.'

'Has it helped?' Amba was more than curious.

'The ghost appears often but refuses to tell her origins or her wishes and only abuses all of us for ruining the girl's life by trying to get her married. Can you imagine? Marriage ruining a girl's life! What every girl wants the moment she grows up!'

'My Gopal was also possessed at night,' Amba began to tell her own story. As she talked, she noticed that a middle-aged sadhu with closely cropped grey hair and a smooth, clean-shaven face had joined their small group. He squatted silently at its edge, listening intently to the account of Gopal's boyhood trances and the events on the day of his possession. His interest in her son did not make her as uneasy as it would have in case of another member of his tribe. He was not one of those wild-eyed, bearded men with matted hair she had been taught to both fear and regard with awe. So many of them were rogues, preying on the naïve. This one was fine-boned and though small in stature, the aura of calm authority around him, the serenity on his face and the compassion in his eyes inspired confidence that he was a genuine holy man. Reassured, Amba turned away and did not pay him any further attention.

Amba had noticed that the groups in the boarding house were fluid. People wandered in and out of a group depending on how interested they were in a particular story of possession and the progress of its healing at Balaji. As she looked around the courtyard of the boarding house where the cooking fires were dying out and people had begun to disperse for the night, she felt safe, protected and pleasantly tired. In the days to come, she would lose her terror of the ghosts; they assumed individual personalities and became increasingly familiar. She would learn that they were wandering spirits of individuals who had died violent or premature deaths. Longing to be released from their halfway house between life and death, the possessing spirits were not really evil, only angry and desperately unhappy.

The first service of the day was just after sunrise but the lodgers were awake long before that. The temple regulations required a daily morning bath and a fresh change of clothes before a patient and his family members could come before Balaji. Since there were only two water taps to serve the whole boarding house, people would start queuing up in the last part of the night when the moon was still high. By the time they reached the temple, the sun, in a blaze of gold, was just clearing the top of the cliff against which the temple nestled, sending the dawn streaming into the courtyard and down the wide stone steps, washing them in a golden orange glow. The main hall, lit by flares in the corners, was already crowded with more than a hundred people as the possessed and their families patiently awaited their turn.

'You just have to wait till one of the priests asks you to step forward,' the neighbour, who had generously offered to guide Amba through the proceedings, informed her.

Amba nodded, her arm tightening around Gopal's shoulder as she watched the goings on. When nudged forward by a priest, a family member would take the patient by the hand and approach the ochre and silver stone idol of Balaji. They would then offer two *laddoos* to another priest standing behind the iron grill. The priest would touch the sweets to a part of the idol and give them back to the patient. The family would then withdraw to the back of the hall where the patient was cajoled or forced to eat the laddoos. Tense moments followed as the family members and interested onlookers waited to see whether the power of Balaji, incorporated in the laddoos, would force the possessing spirit to surface. The ghost could be stubborn, Amba was told, especially if it was a Muslim spirit, and then it could take the cumulative effect of many more services over the next few days before it was forced to make an appearance.

Clutching the boy's hand and half dragging him behind her, Amba walked around the hall, pausing to stop for a few moments at the edge of groups where a ghost had appeared. For some patients, the ghost's appearance was marked by a rhythmic swaying of the upper half of the body and a violent shaking of the head. In others the advent of the spirit was more terrifying as the patients began to beat the floor with their hands or hit their backs against the wall. A small crowd had gathered around a frail young girl whose ghost was challenging Balaji in a guttural male voice.

'You have called me here,' the ghost was saying, 'but if you have any courage you should come out of the temple and then I'll show you my strength.'

The people gathered around the girl began shouting slogans in praise of the god, further provoking the spirit which now turned abusive.

And then the onlookers joined the battle against the ghost: 'You want to fight Baba, do you? . . . Baba, give him a good thrashing, this villain will never listen otherwise.'

The girl began to hit her thighs and breasts with her knotted fists, as the angry spirit bellowed in protest:

'I shall not submit! I'll see you all in hell first!'

After some time the girl, clearly exhausted, stopped hitting herself. But to the great disappointment of the family and the crowd, just when the spirit was on the verge of admitting defeat, the girl fainted, allowing the ghost to escape.

When it was their turn, Gopal docilely accepted the laddoos from the priest and then allowed himself to be led to one corner of the hall where the three of them sat down. Even after he was coaxed to eat both the laddoos there was no sign of the possessing spirit. After waiting for more than twenty minutes his mother looked at the neighbour in mute disappointment.

'Sometimes it takes more than a month. And there are always a few people whose spirit never makes an appearance,' the woman explained, and noticing Amba's dismay, added, 'Trust in Baba.' An old man, who had walked up to them, waiting for something to happen, yawned and wandered off. Gopal, who had been sitting all this time with his eyes closed and his back against the wall, suddenly opened his eyes, stood up and started to walk towards the exit with a firm stride. His mother was about to stop him when the neighbour held up a warning hand.

'Let him go, sister. A patient may do anything here. Nothing is forbidden. No harm will come to him.'

Amba obeyed and helplessly watched her gentle son with his oddly shaped body turn the corner and disappear into the outer courtyard.

After a few minutes Amba could not restrain herself, and the two women went after the boy. From the top of the steps, they could see Gopal in the lane. He was squatting on the ground with his back to the temple. His shirt and sacred thread were lying next to him in a crumpled heap. As the women came down the steps, Amba saw the sadhu again. He was sitting cross-legged on the lowest step, immobile like a rock in a shallow stream while people eddied around him as they climbed up to the temple. He was watching the boy with intense concentration.

'Don't interfere, no matter what he does,' the neighbour said, adding to Amba's unease caused by the sadhu's mysterious interest in her son.

As the women approached Gopal, they saw him peering into the open gutter that flowed in front of the tea shop. And then, to her horror, Amba saw him carefully pick up a leaf plate from the sluggish sludge that carried children's pee, vegetable peelings, orange rinds and other refuse. He licked the leftovers from the leaf plate and then place it on the top of his head before throwing it back into the gutter. When the next leaf plate came bobbing on the filthy water, he repeated the same ritual. Except for the two women and the sadhu, no one else seemed to pay the boy the slightest attention. For a curious spectator there were other, more interesting exhibits: a middle-aged man lying prostrate on the ground with his face down, his arms stretched out above his head and palms joined together, propelling himself forward on the ground a couple of inches at a time with the help of his elbows; a small boy on all fours like a dog, being led by his parents with a chain around his neck; an elderly couple trying to restrain their daughter, a young woman screaming obscenities as she tried to tear off her blouse. But Amba had eyes only for her son and his ritual with the leaf plates which he went on repeating till she could no longer bear it. Unmindful of the neighbour's remonstrances, she walked up to Gopal and picked up his shirt and sacred thread. Gopal had turned to her with a blissful expression on his face. Gently, she extended her hand to her poor, possessed son. Looking straight ahead and without a backward glance at the temple, she led him back to the boarding house.

In the next three days, although the number of laddoos offered to the temple deities was increased and the more expensive *burfi* added to the offerings, Gopal's ghost did not appear even once during the morning and evening services for Balaji or the afternoon service for Pret-raja. Gopal would eat the laddoos without protest, patiently await the ghost's appearance and then wander out into the street to continue his private rituals. He had added a new task to his routine—keeping the area around the temple clean, especially of cattle dung and dog shit. He would wait till a dog had finished and then rush up to scoop the still warm turds in his hands, sending the frightened dog scampering away. Bearing the dog shit in triumph to the gutter that ran along the lane, he would deposit it in the water with the solemnity of a devotee offering flowers to a sacred river. The only change in his condition was a marked increase in his need for sleep. Besides a long afternoon nap, he went to sleep immediately after an early dinner and had to be roughly shaken awake so as to be in time for the morning service. His mother usually chatted for a while with the neighbour after dinner and often both the women would join other groups of patients and their families. Here the most intimate details of the individual's distress were revealed, speculations on the probable origins of the possessing spirit advanced, and the possible outcome of a particular healing ritual debated. The daily bulletins on the antics of various spirits—what they said and how they behaved during their appearance— reassured Amba that however stubborn Gopal's ghost seemed to be, it, too, would soon appear and submit to Balaji's authority after appropriate negotiations.

She did not see the sadhu at these evening gatherings. During the day, though, when she came out after the morning service, she would find him sitting in the same place on the temple steps, watching Gopal. She no longer found his interest in her son sinister. By the third day, she felt familiar enough to respectfully salute him with folded hands, a greeting he acknowledged by slightly inclining his head and raising his right hand in benediction.

Sheela's ghost finally admitted her origins and the neighbour was highly pleased. The breakthrough came one afternoon at the end of the service for Pret-raja. As always, the ghost had appeared but declined to identify herself. Disappointed, the mother was about to leave when someone suggested that she try approaching a minor god—an assistant of the god of death and responsible for taking the soul to the world of ancestral spirits—who had his dwelling place in the courtyard on the second floor. This god was not important enough to have either an idol or a separate priest. His presence was marked merely by a small marble platform on which boiled rice, dal and other edibles from the offerings made by the devout were heaped. Stray dogs and street urchins were gathered around the heap, rushing in to snatch the delicacies—laddoos or burfis—when a fresh offering was added to the mound. As the mount of the god of death, a dog was sacrosanct in the temple precincts. Slightly higher than the marble platform and towards its left was a water cistern which was the favourite bathing place of the stray dogs. Patients were expected to drink from this cistern to show their faith in the god and to cause discomfiture to the possessing spirit. After Sheela had drunk a mouthful of the dirty water, she fell to the ground in a trance and the spirit identified herself for the first time.

'Imagine!' the mother said. 'It was Sheela's aunt! The woman killed herself when Sheela was three years old.'

'Suicide?' Amba was shocked.

The neighbour's loud and contented sigh announced her eagerness to tell the story. The children were asleep in their rooms. Exhausted from the afternoon's exertions, Sheela had gone straight to bed after her return from the temple while Gopal, who could barely keep his eyes open during dinner, was lost to the conscious world.

'She was the wife of my husband's elder brother,' the neighbour began, 'and was thirty years old when she died. She liked men, you know. Liked them too much. We women knew about her affairs and her habit of taking lovers indiscriminately from all castes, including the low-caste labourers who worked in our family's beedi-making enterprise. We begged her to stop, warned her of the dangers, but she was like a runaway horse who could not stop. My brother-in-law was unaware of his wife's amorous adventures till one day he caught her in the act with one of the labourers and there was a violent quarrel between the couple. She killed herself the same night.

'Now the spirit claims that it was not suicide but murder. That her husband strangled her and then made it look as if she had hanged herself. She wants the whole family to ask for forgiveness in a special puja before she will consent to leave my daughter and go to the world of ancestral spirits where she belongs. It is over now. We can all go home.'

With Gopal's ghost adamantly refusing to reveal itself and deprived of the neighbour's cheerful support on which she had come to depend, Amba began to lose heart. She still attended the daily services at the temple, carried out all the prescribed rituals and dutifully washed her son's smeared and stinking hands after his street-cleaning labours. But the fervently told tales about the power of Balaji and the miraculous cures the god had effected could no longer keep the voice of her doubt from becoming insistent. They had been in Mehndipur for over a week and it now seemed to her that the gods had foresaken her and her unfortunate son. She was deciding on a day for their departure when one afternoon, as she was coming down the temple steps, the sadhu came up to her. Again, she was impressed by the dignity with which he carried himself, the space around him an island of peace amidst the surrounding noise and squalor.

'Daughter, you want to go back home,' he said. It was a statement, not a question.

She was not surprised that he knew. The prescience of sadhus was something she took for granted.

'The boy cannot be cured of possession simply because he is not possessed by a spirit,' he continued.

'But, Maharaj,' she said, 'everyone says his madness is the result of possession. The astrologer . . .'

The sadhu shook his head.

'They are mistaken,' he said, with a finality that did not allow any questions or discussion.

'The sadhu told my mother that my madness was not caused by a ghost or a demon as the astrologer had diagnosed,' Gopal later told his disciples. 'It was inspired by the gods. If I was mad then it was the madness of saints. He explained to her that my bizarre actions came from uncontrolled surges of devotion. I was so brimming over with the love of God, so full of anxious desire for His vision, that conventions of normal behaviour could not hold back the longing flooding my soul. Without freedom from the bondages of hate, fear, shame, vanity, disgust, the pride of noble descent and obsession with formal good conduct, no one can truly embark on a spiritual journey. In my madness I was freeing myself from some of these bonds. By throwing away my sacred thread I was throwing away my pride of descent as a Brahmin. The rituals with the leaf plates and dog droppings were intended to break the shackles of disgust and shame. Of course, with the end of my madness, all the bondages which our conditioning forges reasserted themselves. It took many years of hard work and spiritual discipline to permanently break their hold on my mind.'

'Daughter,' the sadhu said, 'there is no other way out of his illness. The boy is destined to be a sadhu, perhaps even a great Paramahamsa. Gift him to us. Let him come with me to our monastery. God willing, you will see him again.'

Amba was stunned.

For three days she hoped and prayed. She was one of the first to enter the temple when its massive teak doors opened at dawn and among the last to leave when they closed at night. She no longer let Gopal leave her side, dragging him from one ritual to another, badgering the priests to intercede with Balaji more often on her son's behalf. She doubled the number of laddoos in the offering at the morning service, making up for the extra expense by foregoing vegetables for the evening meal and eating the rice with a thin, watery dal. All this time she struggled to keep the fast-fading hope alive that Gopal was possessed by a ghost and not by God as the sadhu had claimed.

Deprived of his daily ritual with the leaf plates and dog shit, Gopal again became apathetic and withdrawn, his eyes emptying of the light his obsession had given them. On the fourth day he did not get out of bed. Amba entreated, cajoled, scolded but Gopal remained silently obdurate. Around noon, he began to quietly weep, the tears flowing down his face till the ducts ran dry. Amba's anxious queries were met with silence.

By the evening, when the cooking fires were being lit in the dharamshala, Amba had admitted defeat. They had not eaten the whole day and even now as the cooking smells wafted in, Amba made no move to get up and prepare dinner. She kept sitting in the dark room, next to her son who lay huddled on a mat, perhaps weeping again. She sensed rather than saw the sadhu at the door.

'Take him, Maharaj,' she said without turning her head. 'If he will go with you.'

'Oh, don't worry, daughter, he will come,' the sadhu said, breaking her heart.

Chapter Seven

Dusk had begun to settle in small increments of leaden darkness when the boy and the old sadhu finally arrived at the monastery. In spite of a three-hour jolty bus ride on a road scarred with pot holes, and a five-mile walk on a hilly path which provided the only access to the narrow valley of Galta, the sadhu seemed fresh and rested. Although he had rarely spoken, only murmuring '*Hari Ram*' under his breath every once in a while, he had often smiled at Gopal, giving him looks of sympathetic interest throughout the bus journey. The boy had not spoken a word since the morning when he fetched him from the dharamshala. But he was definitely livelier than yesterday and, as the sadhu had known, had followed him docilely to the tonga stand at the end of the bazaar. He seemed to have transferred all his apathy to his mother who remained stony-faced and dry-eyed, incapable of even feeling despair, as she watched her son climb into the tonga and set off on the first leg of the journey to Galta.

As they passed through the gate now, the sadhu put a protective arm around the boy's shoulder and pointed to the monastery on the rocky hill in front of them.

'That is where you will live,' he said, and added, 'with me.'

Hemmed in from three sides by bare hills, straight-backed against the sky, the Galta complex, of which the monastery was a part, consisted of temples, bathing ghats and resting pavilions for pilgrims who came in large numbers to take a dip in the water tanks at the time of solar and lunar eclipses. The complex straddled three levels, climbing up the middle hill like terraced fields in mountainous land. The sprawling ruins of the old monastery, the garden, the five Rama and Krishna temples built by various kings of Jaipur, and the large bathing tank for women were at the ground level. A steep flight of steps led up to smaller temples and a deep tank for men at the middle level. At the uppermost level was a small reservoir, connected to the water tanks and fed by a perennial spring that emerged through an opening in the hill in the shape of a cow's mouth. There was also a small, white marble Sun temple next to the reservoir. It had an open courtyard lined with a dozen rooms in a state of utter disrepair. A narrow path winding up the hill amid stubble and stones led from the Sun temple to the new monastery, built ten years back, less than half a mile away. At the time of Gopal's arrival, the monastery housed thirty-two ascetics of the Ramanandi sect.

The monastery at Galta was the legacy of Krishnadas, known as Pavahari ('one who lives on air') Baba, a famous ascetic who came to the area that was to become Jaipur at the beginning of the sixteenth century. He selected a cave in the inhospitable wilds of Galta on the eastern outskirts of the present city of Jaipur for the practice of his Yogic austerities and meditations. At the time, Galta was inhabited by a sect of tantriks feared for their magical prowess. In the ensuing duel of supernatural powers, Pavahari Baba succeeded in vanquishing the tantriks and driving them away. The only problem with Galta, otherwise ideal for ascetic meditation, was its lack of water. Pavahari Baba had to fly every afternoon to the Ganga, hundreds of miles away, for his daily bath. One day, while meditating on his chosen deity, Lord Rama, Pavahari Baba was blessed with a vision of the God.

'Do you need anything, Pavahari?' the Lord asked.

'How can I lack for anything as long as I have You, my Lord!' Pavahari Baba replied.

Then as the god was about to fold back his vision and vanish, the ascetic added:

'Well, maybe one thing. It is inconvenient to fly to the Ganga for a bath every afternoon. Perhaps if the Ganga could come here?'

Rama instantly granted the boon and the water of the Ganga began to gush out of the side of the hill.

In 1504, Pavahari Baba, who was a Ramanandi sadhu, founded a monastery at the same spot. In the following centuries, temples and bathing tanks for pilgrims were added with the support of the Jaipur durbar and the barons of the state, making Galta the most important Ramanandi centre in north India. Its present *mahant*, sixteenth in the line of succession to Pavahari Baba, was Madhavacharya, Gopal's companion.

A few goats wandered on the gravelled paths between the temples, competing with the monkeys for the peanuts, roasted gram and the occasional banana thrown by the pious to feed the animals. The struggle for food was half-hearted, occasioned less by hunger than by a need to maintain a hierarchical order established by the goats which was often challenged by the monkeys. As they climbed up the steps leading to the monastery, Gopal and Madhavacharya passed a goat making its way up to the men's tank, keeping a wary eye on the monkey at its side who was engaged in the same endeavour but was careful to remain well out of the reach of the goat's stubby but sharp horns.

The dusk worship was over and most of the ascetics were gathered in the assembly hall for the evening meal when Madhavacharya and Gopal entered the monastery. From the monastery's puja room, a large hall with a white marble floor at the end of which stood two four-feet-high, gold-plated, flower-bedecked statues of Rama and Sita, came the sound of male voices singing to the accompaniment of a harmonium and the rhythmic beat of brass bells.

'The *kirtan* has been going on day and night, unbroken for the last four hundred years,' Madhavacharya said. 'There are always two monks who are on singing duty and the singers are replaced every hour. Others may join in whenever they are free.'

Gopal stopped for a moment, listening.

'I like to sing,' he said, his first words since they boarded the bus at Mehndipur.

'You shall. As often as you want to,' Madhavacharya

said, welcoming the birth of light in the boy's eyes.

In Madhavacharya's room, the kerosene lantern hanging from a nail in the wall spread a pale yellow light over the meagre furnishings: a wooden cot covered with a thin mattress and a coarse sheet; a low stool next to the bed; a chipped teak desk in a corner with two thick, cloth-covered tomes and a pair of wire-rimmed spectacles lying on it; a worn bamboo mat that covered one-fourth of the floor. Two white robes and a towel were neatly folded and stacked on a shelf built inside the wall. A bronze statue from Mysore, six inches high, depicting Rama as a child—Ram-lalla—stood on the window sill just above the bed, and next to it was a small earthen plate containing two marigold flowers and a stick of dhoop.

Madhavacharya motioned Gopal to sit on the mat at the foot of the bed. Two young ascetics, barely a couple of years older than Gopal, entered the room. One carried a bucket of water, and the other a plate of bananas in one hand and a hookah in the other which he placed on the floor next to the bed. After touching the mahant's feet they squatted down on the floor and began to wash his feet. Madhavacharya peeled the bananas.

'Eat,' he said to Gopal.

Another monk entered the room with the monastery's account book bound in red cloth.

'Ah, Vishnu Das!' Madhavacharya's voice had none of the warmth with which he had blessed the young monks.

Vishnu Das, a tall, thin man in his mid-forties with a gaunt, bearded face and deep-set eyes, touched Madhavacharya's feet in perfunctory respect.

'I trust you had a good trip,' he said.

'Yes,' Madhavacharya answered shortly and began to smoke the hookah, drawing on it noisily.

'And the purpose for which you deprived us of your presence for so many days was also fulfilled?'

'Yes.'

'Can we go through the accounts? I also have some bad news. About Charan Das. You remember? I had warned you about him.'

'Not today, Vishnu, I am tired. I am sure you looked after the monastery admirably in my absence. Tomorrow.'

And then noticing Vishnu Das looking at Gopal, he added, 'He will be living with us.'

'Is he the one?'

'Yes. I have a strong intuition about this boy.'

Vishnu Das gave Gopal another cold look that lingered on the swell of his breasts for a second before it returned to Madhavacharya. He smiled faintly.

'Tomorrow, then,' he said, and nodded to the young monks.

After the ascetics left, Madhavacharya opened the window, blew out the lantern, and gently lifted the statue of Ram-lalla into his lap. A wave of tenderness washed over his face, smoothening the creases that had appeared while he spoke to Vishnu Das. He began his nightly meditation with a contemplation of Rama as his infant son. His soft features became softer as his absorption into his motherhood deepened. With his eyes closed, he began to rock back and forth, crooning gently over the metallic child, his voice suffused with mother-love.

Gopal lay on the mat, listening to Madhavacharya's murmured lullaby. He closed his own eyes, and sensed the presence of his mother in the room. Suddenly, there was a tug deep inside his body. He felt something heavy shift, lurch within him. A thin film of moisture began to coat his eyes, heralding an agonizing wrench in a heart long forbidden grief. He wept quietly, his sobs no more than a rustling of leaves in a rush of wind. And then his head was lifted tenderly onto the sadhu's lap. The sorrow that had lain heavily upon his breast trembled and retreated, releasing him from its black embrace. Warm fingers caressed his forehead, patted his wet cheeks and a tobacco-laden breath blew lightly over him as he slept.

An hour before dawn, when the cold silver moon still hung high in a slate-coloured sky, Gopal was awakened by the sounds of the monastery stirring to life. He was alone in the room. Like many older ascetics, Madhavacharya preferred to begin his morning meditation in the last quarter of the night when the silence of the hills was undisturbed by early morning bird calls and the coughing of monkeys who lived in the trees around the temples. Some ascetics were bathing in the men's tank, getting ready for the first of the day's four *aartis*. After the early morning worship, they would disperse till the midday meal: most to fulfil the responsibilities of sweeping, cleaning, cooking, gardening and other tasks which kept the monastery and their collective lives running smoothly, some to join in the kirtan or sit around in the temples chatting with lay devotees, and others to study the *Ramayana* and other sacred texts in their rooms. The afternoons were free, to be structured as an ascetic pleased. Most sat with their friends, joking and talking about the day's events and gossiping about monastery politics. A few invited their friends to their rooms for some serious ganja smoking.

The blowing of the conch shell, announcing the birth of another dawn, summoned the monks to the Sun temple. Gopal sat on a rock midway between the monastery and the temple, watching their visitor from the previous evening, the bearded monk Vishnu Das, officiate at the worship of the Sun-god. Above the spire, he could see the heavy sun lifting itself bit by bit above the hill, hastening the disappearance of the wan moon, stirring warmth into the vastness of the sky. Below, Vishnu Das had begun the aarti to welcome the fiery deity. He stood facing the altar with a five-pronged lamp in his right hand. Moving his right arm before him, he drew seven circles in the air, faint rings of fire in front of the idol of the Sun-god, while with his left hand he rang a brass bell. The other monks chanted hymns to the Sun and his daughter, Usha, the Dawn, and Vishnu Das repeated the same motions with an incense holder containing three sticks of slow-burning incense. Led by Madhavacharya, the ascetics then trooped back to the puja hall where another aarti was offered to the monastery's tutelary deities, Rama and Sita. Here the atmosphere was much livelier. Some monks sang along with the designated kirtan singers. Others danced about the altar, circling clockwise and chanting the mantra—

Hari Krishna, Hari Krishna, Krishna, Krishna, Hari, Hari
Hari Rama, Hari Rama, Rama, Rama, Hari, Hari.

As the dancing became ecstatic, more and more monks joined the circle till it ended with the last sweep of Vishnu Das's fly whisk when everyone knelt down to receive the Divine couple's grace. The dancers were perspiring, their elated exhaustion confirming their belief that Lord Vishnu in his avatars of Rama and Krishna had sung and danced with them. Trays filled with bananas and sliced cucumbers were first offered to the deities and then distributed among the monks as their breakfast, which was followed by several cups of hot tea.

Within a week of his arrival in Galta, Gopal was fully recovered. Except for sorely missing his mother during the first few weeks, he was back to his normal state of mind, to the time before he had met the tantrik. So many baffling, even fatal illnesses are inexplicably cured in hospitals and healing temples, in doctors' offices and the shrines of holy men, that Gopal's sudden freedom from his affliction, whether caused by ghost or God, cannot really be called a miracle, not even a minor one. Gopal accepted the disappearance of whatever had enthralled his soul as matter-of-factly as did Madhavacharya. But with the return of normalcy also came the return of normal emotions. Although Madhavacharya only saw him at nights, his homesickness was not difficult to divine. The mahant decided to deal with it not by the slow workings of empathy but by the radical method of a scolding, though a gentle one.

'How can you ever hope to be a sadhu! Not to speak of

becoming a Paramahamsa! Putting on the ochre robe of a monk will not make one a monk if there is no detachment. You are a sadhu only if you feel the world is like a forest fire, if you regard your family as a deep well, your parents as roaring tigers. You may weep, but for God alone. *That* is real detachment!'

Despite the homesickness, Gopal took easily to the daily routine of the monastery. He rose before four in the morning while it was still dark and finished bathing before most of the other monks came down to the tank. He was self-conscious about his breasts and took care that they remained hidden under the loose yellow shift worn by young ascetics waiting for their initiation into the order. The formal obligations on an ascetic—although Gopal had not been initiated as one—were minimal. There were the aartis—the two morning ones, followed by one at noon and the last after sunset—that Gopal had to participate in. Together with other inmates of the monastery, visiting ascetics and lay devotees, he ate the mid-day meal of fried puris, fresh yogurt and two seasonal vegetables and the evening dinner of rice and dal in the assembly hall. His duties, too, were less than arduous. Unlike the ascetics whose responsibilities kept on shifting from day to day, Madhavacharya had assigned him the work of sweeping the puja hall and the Hanuman temple below Pavahari Baba's cave. Gopal had wanted to attend the Sanskrit school where newly initiated monks learnt to read and recite sacred texts, but Madhavacharya had unaccountably refused permission.

'It will only muddy your clarity,' he had said cryptically.

After finishing his work in the morning, Gopal wandered

around the complex, visiting different temples, watching the pilgrims, not as a spectator but as a silent participant in their devotion. He also liked to climb up to the cave where Pavahari Baba had meditated. It was small and dark, smelt of bats, and one could neither lie down nor stand up it, only sit cross-legged in the lotus posture. Gopal would close his eyes and imagine he was the great ascetic himself, meditating on the divine form of Lord Rama who before long would grace him with a vision. He spent his afternoon and much of the evening in the puja hall, singing. It was not just the depth of feeling he put into the songs that induced more and more pilgrims to make the short climb up to the monastery to hear the gifted singer. What they heard but only dimly sensed were echoes of a music vibrant with an other-worldly beauty; as if the melodiousness of his voice was not his alone and that within him sang another who dwelt infinitely nearer to the Lord. With each day that passed, Gopal felt the devotional fervour of his singing increase, as if the very floor and walls of the hall, conserving memories of old ecstasies, were pulling him further and further towards *mahabhava*, the divinely inspired 'great feeling' that Madhavacharya so often talked about at night when they were alone in his room.

Chapter Eight

The Ramanandi ascetics had their beginning as a devotional sect in the fifteenth century when bhakti cults mushroomed all over the country. The Ramanandi spiritual discipline comprised primarily devotion to Rama through the cultivation of one of the five spiritual moods, or *bhavas,* through which the ascetics sought to establish a relationship with the Divine. One could strive for the emotional state of Rama's servant, friend, or parent, or one could approach the Lord through the serenity of *shanta* or through the *madhura bhava* of the lover.

'You can express your love for God through any one of these moods,' Madhavacharya explained to Gopal during the instructions he gave the boy over the next few months. 'Hold fast to a form you especially like—the Lord as master, friend, child or even lover. Keep this form bright and vivid before your eyes all the time. "I am his servant", "I am His friend"—these expressions contain the ripe "I", the "I" of spiritual knowledge. "I am a Brahmin", "I am the son of so and so", "I am rich", "I am poor"—these have the "I" of ignorance that strengthens the bonds of ego and pride. This "I" binds you to the world and must be renounced if you are to lead a life of the spirit. At Balaji, I knew at first glance that you were a born renouncer, someone who had reached the highest state of non-attachment in your previous birth.'

As he got more and more absorbed in a bhava, Madhavacharya said, the devotee's consciousness of the external world diminished, his awareness of the body dimmed. Depending upon the intensity of his contemplation, the internal current of a particular spiritual mood could become so strong that finally the chosen form of God became manifest. The devotee saw the form standing before him. It smiled, it moved, it spoke to him, as if it were palpably alive. The full experience of a bhava, where the mind was empty of all thought and feeling except the bhava itself, would lead to the ecstatic state of mystical absorption, the *savikalpa samadhi*.

'Here the "I" does not completely disappear in the Divine, as in the *nirvikalpa samadhi*,' Madhavacharya explained to the boy. 'A thin line, barely a trace, remains to enjoy the presence of the Lord. There is an exultation that takes one outside life. The body is racked with unexpected waves of pleasure, so much so that one can scarcely bear the weight of this reward.'

The madhura bhava, the spiritual mood of being God's lover, according to the mahant, contained the essence of all other moods. It was also the most difficult. In Krishna worship, for instance, the devotee needed to recreate the feeling-state of Radha within himself. The teachers advised against this attempt. They maintained that only the bhava of Radha's girlfriend was attainable, not that of Krishna's beloved. The difference between the two, though only of a degree and not of a kind, was vital. Radha was another man's wife and her longing for Krishna, imbued with the riotous force of illicit and adulterous passion, always threatened to contaminate her spiritual striving with lust. Madhura should have all the qualities of erotic love—except the carnal.

Madhavacharya maintained that the practice of madhura was easier for a Ramanandi ascetic since he did not have to imitate the storms in Radha's soul but recreate within himself the quieter, gentler love of Sita for Rama, her husband. Yet he, too, had to transcend the biology of his male body, become female in his emotional response to God. For the consciousness of having a body and the firm conviction that one was a 'man' or a 'woman' were the two fundamental building blocks of the human mind. When the male aspirant was able to transcend his maleness by becoming a wife to the Lord, he had freed himself from one of the two shackles of nature and was very near a state that was beyond all bhavas. A woman devotee had it only apparently easier. She could continue to retain her body but the urge for union with Krishna or Rama mobilized all her natural female sexuality, thus endangering the bhava.

The majority of Ramanandi ascetics had always expressed their devotion to Rama through a cultivation of the servant bhava. They had tried to incorporate the attitude and mental state of Hanuman, the epitome of devoted service to the god. The parental bhava was confined to a small number of generally very senior ascetics, such as Madhavacharya himself, who had the courage to regard Rama as their son and seat him in the lap.

The erotic mood where the devotee put on female clothes

and ornaments and, identifying with Sita, behaved like a wife
to the deity, had always been rare, except for a few years in
the eighteenth century. Influenced by the poetry of Tulsi Das
who describes the amorous life of the Divine Couple in his
Uttara Kand, Madhuracharya, who was the mahant of Galta
at the time, encouraged the erotic worship of Rama, leading
to some scandalous behavior among supposedly celibate
monks as they tried to imitate the joyful amours of Rama and
Sita. Partly as a reaction to the excesses of those turbulent
years which required the intervention of the ruler, Jai Singh,
the founder of the city of Jaipur, a more austere worship
comprising Yogic practice, textual study and recitation of the
Ramayana became the dominant mode of Ramanandi
spiritual life. The original ecstatic impulse, though, never
completely disappeared. And it was the complaint of Vishnu
Das and other senior ascetics that Madhavacharya was
attempting to revive the bhava worship of his
eighteenth-century predecessor, with its very real danger of a
distasteful, and ultimately disastrous, emotionalism.

In an assembly of the senior-most monks, called a few
days before he left for Mehndipur, Madhavacharya had
protested.

'No one has ever reached the other shore by poring over
books. What is the sense in reading about Him, intellectually
pondering over His mysteries, if you cannot feel the vigour of
His name? We can only think by feeling, my brothers. The
saddest fate for an ascetic is to suffer a passion that is wholly
of the mind, to have thoughts that are divorced from sinews
and bone, to experience ecstasies that are not of the blood
but of the head alone.'

'Your eloquence is legendary, elder brother,' Vishnu Das had replied coldly. 'But we have to learn to walk before we can run. Most of us are poor mortals, fated to spend our lives crawling toward Rama. What you seek to encourage is an overreaching that can only plunge our frail minds into darkness rather than illuminate them. What will be left is madness . . . and scandal.'

Now, on his return from Mehndipur, Madhavacharya found that the older monks were still simmering. They were particularly unhappy about the case of Charan Das, which they saw as the latest instance in a disturbing trend that the mahant was actively sponsoring.

Madhavacharya had just finished checking the monastery accounts one evening and was going through his correspondence when Charan Das was brought in. Small and thin, with a wizened face and a mouth lacking much of its full complement of teeth, Charan Das looked at least a decade older than his fifty-odd years. Still wearing a long crimson skirt and a short bright yellow blouse tied at the back with a single string, the old monk fairly cackled with good humour as he was escorted into the mahant's office by Vishnu Das.

'Ah, friend, Rama be praised that you are back. These fellows are trying to stop me from going to the Lord,' Charan Das said, giving the grim-faced Vishnu Das standing beside him a withering look.

'Elder brother refuses to take off the woman's clothes he has been wearing for the last fortnight. He also insists on bathing in the women's tank,' Vishnu Das reported.

'Where else will I bathe but in the women's tank!' Charan Das was shocked by the implied suggestion. 'It will be a sad day for Galta and the certain end of virtue if men and women started to bathe together. Ah, Madhav, my brother, you cannot imagine my state, how my heart is brimming over with love for the Lord! He may come any moment and take me into his arms.'

'You are indeed blessed, brother Charan,' Madhavacharya said gravely. 'But Rama will not seek you out if you wander around in the temples among the worldly. Pray and wait for him in solitude in your room or in a secluded corner of the monastery garden.'

'You are wise, Madhav. But how can your wisdom be intelligble to these young men who neither know of the spirit nor have lived the full range of life? What do they know of the longings of Sita's heart which my tongue cannot utter?' Charan Das said, and again looked scornfully at the impassive Vishnu Das.

'Do try and understand, Vishnu,' Madhavacharya tried to placate his glowering deputy after the old monk left. 'Love can never be base, even when it overflows its banks. It may sometimes be misdirected but one never knows when and where it will find the right channel. Wasn't the revered Goswami Tulsi Das so infatuated with his young wife that he could not bear her absence for a single moment? Did he not follow her around the house like a dog, or with his eyes like a baby when they were in the same room? And then, one day, his inner eye suddenly opened when she said to him, "If you hungered for Rama as fiercely as you do for me, you would have attained salvation long ago." All his love and its urgent cravings now became directed towards Rama. The Lord's grace flowed into him and Goswami spent the rest of his life composing the glorious verses of Rama's story.'

'That was a long time ago, elder brother,' Vishnu Das retorted. 'The world has changed since then and with it, men. It is nice to muse about the saints but disastrous to imitate them. Let us savour the past without trying to regain it.'

One year passed. Gopal's breasts shrank. They were no longer so prominent against his thin chest. They were like the breasts of a twelve-year-old girl in the first flush of youth, a size they were to retain for the rest of his life. Gopal was now a part of the community of ascetics although his status within it was ambiguous. No one had seen him wearing the six-yard-long sacred thread but most assumed that he was going through the two-year observation period prior to his initiation in the Ramanandi order. Initially, the fact that he slept in the mahant's room had excited envy and shocked comment among the younger ascetics. Also, he preferred solitude and did not participate in the afternoon banter and gossip, and this was misinterpreted by many as arrogance. But his guileless nature, his cheerful willingness to run errands—fetching cigarettes and chewing tobacco from the grocery shop outside the temple complex for anyone who asked—and a total absence of any sign of favouritism by the mahant, soon endeared him to most monks. Not to Vishnu Das, of course, although he, too, grudgingly acknowledged the boy's rare musical gift that was drawing more and more devotees to the monastery's kirtan singing.

Vishnu Das had not believed the mahant's story about

the dream that had led him to Gopal. A few months ago, Madhavacharya had called his deputy to his room and after swearing him to secrecy, narrated his dream of the previous night. Madhavacharya had dreamt of a boy standing on a cliff, crying 'Father! Father!!' while a gale-like wind howled around him.

'It was the soul of a saint. I know it was. The boy's body had all the signs of a pure and free soul—lightness of limb, softness of bone. He was calling out to me, Vishnu, and I must go and look for him.'

'Where?'

'I recognized the cliff. It's the one in Mehndipur, the one with the Balaji temple at its foot. Besides, the force of the wind provides another clue: Balaji is the son of the god of winds.'

Vishnu Das had kept quiet. He had always regarded Madhavacharya as a naïve man with a certain poetic elegance to his speech but utterly lacking in common sense. Now that he had seen the peculiar boy, Vishnu Das was confirmed in his opinion about Madhavacharya. The man really was not fit to be the mahant of Galta. Treating an illiterate rustic boy as if he was a saint! What kind of example did it set for other novices who were supposed to spend years studying the scriptures! Saints like Kabir or Ramakrishna who regarded learning as an obstacle to holiness did so from emotion, not knowledge. Was Shankara less holy for being the most learned monk of his age? If allowed to remain at the helm of Galta's affairs Madhavacharya would one day bring it grief. He would ruin it as a centre of learning. What the monastery needed, Vishnu Das was convinced, was to get out of its medieval mindset and enter the modern world. India was on the verge of independence. Now that the war was almost over, the British would soon leave. With their departure the inevitable question would arise: 'Who among us shall have power here, in these villages, in these towns?' The monasteries could help in shaping an answer. They commanded respect all over the country, among all but a handful of Hindus—the brown sahibs—who had embraced the European ways of their conquerors. They could unite a people hopelessly divided into castes and sects around the fundamentals of their ancient religion. They could play a crucial role in knitting the Hindus together into a purposeful and powerful nation which would revive India's ancient glory. Vishnu Das was already in touch with like-minded monks in other monasteries in the United and Central Provinces of British India. But these contacts, through letters carried by wandering sadhus, were still preliminary, involving an exchange of ideas and information rather than any plans of action.

If Vishnu Das's grand hopes were to be fulfilled, the very nature of a monastery like Galta had to change. It could no longer be a mere purveyor of a sentimental religiosity which sapped manliness, weakened a man's fibre and made his soul at once effeminate and that of a slave. Each monk had to be made aware of his vital role in awakening national consciousness and making men out of a people who had been slaves for over a thousand years. 'It is a man-making religion that we want!' Swami Vivekananda had thundered, and Vishnu Das agreed. The Swami, not the adolescent infatuated with the crazy Ramakrishna but the confident adult asserting Hindu civilizational superiority, was his ideal. But for the Swami's vision to be realized people like Madhavacharya had to give way to people like him. Vishnu Das did not want stories about reincarnated saints or God-intoxicated boys coming out of Galta and circulating among the credulous, a description that unfortunately applied to almost all Hindus. Vishnu Das was proud of his religion but ashamed of those who shared his faith—a people always eager to endow the mundane with the miraculous, constantly on the look out for evidence of the transcendental in the ordinary.

What Vishnu Das wanted was stories that would undermine the mahant's position, not strengthen it. The boy would be a hero in the first set of stories but at least a villain's accomplice in the second. That was why when an uncertain Madhavacharya had asked his advice on the propriety of the boy sleeping in his room, Vishnu Das had hastened to reassure him.

'You are like a father to him, elder brother. Where is the question of impropriety! Let him stay in your room. I shall talk to the others. Of course, without revealing the secret of your dream.'

Vishnu Das knew he had to hurry with his plans for replacing Madhavacharya once he saw the effect Gopal's singing had begun to have on some of Galta's lay supporters. One of these was Sitaram Dhamani, a leading Jaipur jeweller and a generous contributor to Galta's coffers. He was also a close friend of Madavacharya's. People found the friendship between two such different men—in looks, temperament and interests—difficult to fathom. Madhavacharya was small,

fine-boned and fair-complexioned. He wore a freshly
laundered white dhoti every morning that retained its
well-ironed folds till the time he went to bed at night. His
ash-and-sandalwood-paste *tilak* was drawn with the skill of
a minaturist, its two vertical lines on the forehead curving
perfectly to meet at the bridge of his nose. He talked softly,
his voice generally a soothing murmur. Dhamani, in total
contrast, was stout, with a dark complexion and a
pock-marked face rescued from ugliness by his overpowering
vitality. The black cap he always wore was ridged with layers
of old hair oil. His crumpled kurta, with its flashy diamond
buttons, was usually spattered with betel-stained spittle and
yellow turmeric spots from the crumbs of the spicy *kachoris*
he consumed throughout the day. Whenever he sat down, his
dhoti rode up his legs, above his fat knees. He scratched his
groin while he talked and was in the habit of nonchalantly
raising a hip to produce a kachori-scented fart. He was also
loyal, emotional and deeply devout, regarding his every visit
to Galta as a small step up an infinitely tall and steep ladder
to salvation.

Madhavcharya was very fond of the jeweller. He
appreciated Dhamani's generosity and relied on his advice in
matters concerning the monastery's finances. Even though
Dhamani clearly looked up to the mahant, Madhavcharya
always treated him as an affectionate friend and never
showed any signs of superiority; he knew that subordination
and friendship are not compatible.

Dhamani had heard of Gopal from Madhavacharya one
afternoon about a month after the boy's arrival at Galta. The
two friends were sitting in the mahant's office. As usual,

Dhamani was regaling Madhavcharya with gossip from the outside world. In Jaipur, the hottest rumour in the bazaar was that Atal, the finance minister, had received a large bribe from a contractor for the construction of the new university. It was also public knowledge that Atal had diverted funds from the department of public works for the new palace that the Maharaja was building for his third wife. Outside Jaipur, one heard that the war was going well for the British. This was a pity. Like many other orthodox Hindus Dhamani liked what he had heard of Hitler. The German dictator was a pious man who ate *sattvic*, vegetarian food. He had put the swastika, the ancient Vedic sign for the sun, on his country's flag and under his tutelage the Germans were hearkening back to a distant Aryan past which the Hindus, too, had shared.

'Sitaram,' Madhavacharya interrupted him. 'You must listen to the kirtan in the evening before you return to Jaipur.'

'Ah, yes,' Dhamani said. 'I have heard a great deal about the boy. Is he really as good as people say?'

'Words such as good and bad are to be used for singers, not for him. I tell you, Sitaram, he is singularly blessed, infinitely more than any one of us who have laboured long and humbly in the Lord's fields. For those who have an ear, his songs can cause such turmoil in the mind that it is no longer content to be blind but is compelled to strive toward light.'

'Hm-m-m,' Dhamani murmured, impressed by his friend's impassioned advocacy.

That evening the jeweller heard Gopal sing for the first time.

Come and settle in my mind, O Rama—
The purpose of my life will be fulfilled.

The notes of the song gave Dhamani gooseflesh, as the melody seeped in through the pores of his body and into the remotest crannies of his mind. Dhamani felt a powerful surge of emotion rise up and choke his throat. He stood up, swaying. 'The bhava has touched him!' Madhavacharya observed with surprise. For an instant he thought his stocky friend intended to join the dancing men on the floor. The other kirtan singers had fallen silent long ago, content to let Gopal carry the song alone. Dhamani staggered, his body racked by involuntary shudders, as he walked up to where Gopal was sitting on the raised platform for the singers. He went down on his knees before the boy, his joined palms raised above his head.

'Father!' he said, his voice trembling and his sight blurred by warm tears. 'Father!' he repeated.

From a corner of the room, Vishnu Das watched the scene. He was frowning.

Chapter Nine

Madhavacharya was restless. Even the ritual seating of Ram-lalla in his lap had not helped his mind concentrate nor brought it peace. While Gopal fell immediately asleep after blowing out the lamp, Madhavacharya lay awake, half listening to the last sounds of the evening taper off into silence. He was aware that the enormous tenderness he generally felt for the boy was rusted with a spot of envy tonight.

He lay in the dark, trying to make sense of his tangled feelings. 'It is so unfair,' he thought. 'It is unfair, Lord. I have devoted my life to You. I have prayed and meditated. I have carried out the required rituals with all the devotion my heart could muster. The craving for You has hollowed out my mind. Yet You refuse to fill it with Your presence. No one knows that behind the composure befitting my age and the calmness people see in my eyes, my soul is like a crazed moth beating against a lit window pane to be let in from the darkness. But the window to Your house remains firmly shut. You choose to bestow Your grace on this boy whom I must love because he has been thus blessed. Oh yes, at least You have granted me the power to see and to hear the signs. I can discern that his music is not merely pleasing to the ear but comes from far away, further than the far side of joy, touching the cusp of chaos where the "I" breaks up into pieces and then reconstitutes itself in Your presence. *That* is not difficult to see. Even Dhamani sensed it. But why choose the boy, Lord? Why not me?'

Madhavacharya turned on his side. It was a moonless night. In the dim light of the stars, he could make out Gopal's huddled shape on the floor. Outside, in the monastery's garden, the raucous cry of a peacock scraped the silence.

'Is it my pride that is at fault, Lord?

'Somewhere, deep within myself, I have always known that the vestige of my pride has not let me fully surrender myself to You. All it has tolerated is submission, and even that brings with it a heaviness of heart. My soul knows it will never partake of the joy that accompanies complete surrender. For though I try to persuade myself to the contrary, remind myself of the example of saints, surrender remains a defeat, not liberation. What holds me back? Perhaps I hesitate because I discern terror in Your beauty. In Your radiant face, Rama, I sometimes catch a glimpse of Kali, the goddess we adore because she refrains from destroying us . . . The boy is indeed blessed. He can surrender—to You, to the song, to the moment, without reservation. For him surrender holds no dread, only joy, even ecstasy.'

A parrot screeched, raging against the stillness of the night.

'I think I understand now—my fate wills that I be like a servant to the boy. I must accompany him on the path to

Your house but forever wait outside the door. O Lord, all that I ever had is long gone. What remains is what I have never had—You. Is the giving up of hope to be my final renunciation? Must I stand completely naked before you? As naked as the day I was born?'

The merest hint of a breeze, no more than an agitation of air, surprisingly soft for this time of the year, came down from the hills and through the window, lightly caressing the old mahant's fevered face. For just a second, he refused to be comforted, resisting the faint cool breath wafting in from the darkness. But then he relaxed, letting go of the last remnants of his future, and slept.

It was in the middle of May, well into the summer of 1946, when Gopal began his spiritual journey at Madhavacharya's behest. The mahant had freed him from his daily chores and monastic obligations but besides the suggestion that he try to recreate the servant bhava of Hanuman within himself, he had refrained from giving any further instructions.

Left on his own, Gopal began by spending the major part of his day in the Hanuman temple. He helped the priest, who was not a monk, in the deity's worship, listened to the lore of the Monkey-god, prayed and sang along with the worshippers. He continued to sweep and swab the temple floor each morning although he was no longer required to do so. In the first week, he went up to the monastery for the aartis and the meals but gradually his attendance at these communal occasions became less frequent, stopping altogether as his immersion in Hanuman deepened. He now spent all his nights in the temple, curled up in a corner on the floor, lying awake till late into the night, thinking of Hanuman, assimilating the essence of the god—his intense longing for Rama.

'Thus the first spiritual discipline I practised,' he would later tell his disciples, 'was not some kind of meditation—that came later—but longing. Some will say longing is not a discipline but a state of the soul. True enough. Yet, longing is the basis of all spiritual life. It must be honed to its highest pitch, through a total immersion in its object, and is thus a meditation after all.'

Absorbed in Hanuman, Gopal found that for long stretches of time he began to forget that he existed separately from the monkey-god.

'At such times,' he recalled, 'my eyes assumed a restless expression like that of a monkey's. I even walked jerkily like one and tried to join one or other of the many troops of monkeys that were dispersed all over the temple complex. At first, the big males chased me off if I came too close but then gradually began to tolerate my presence in their group as long I did not touch a female or a baby. I also spent much of my time in the trees, crying "Rama, Rama!", as Lord Hanuman must have done, beseeching His appearance. Oddly, the lower end of my backbone lengthened by nearly an inch, an incipient tail, although in course of time, when the whole experience was over, it shrank back to its natural size.'

Vishnu Das was secretly pleased though publicly outraged. What was important was that the boy's singing which seemed to have a mesmeric effect on its listeners had stopped. He pretended to be as distressed as the young ascetics who came to him, protesting at the behaviour of the mahant's protégé, and offered to accompany them to Madhavacharya's office as their spokesman.

'The boy has tied a piece of cloth around his waist so that it might look like a tail. Perhaps we should be thankful that he has not cast off all his clothes. He hops around the temples, grubbing out from the dust the berries that people throw to feed the monkeys. That is all he eats now—berries and pieces of fruit.'

'He is not like that all the time,' an older ascetic who was present in the office tried to speak in Gopal's defence. 'If you ask him about this behaviour in his saner moments, he says acting like a monkey is not out of his own accord but that it happens by itself.'

'O Lord, let me stand guard on the road on which the boy is walking toward You. Help me preserve his gift for surrender. Let me be the servant of Your servant,' Madhavacharya said silently to himself before he turned to address the small delegation that had come to his office with the complaint.

'Ah, Vishnu Das, let us remember the tradition of our Order. Let us not forget the vital importance of the servant bhava in our worship. Is there a greater servant of Rama than Lord Hanuman? The soul takes its cues from the body, Vishnu. If the body is a temple, the soul becomes a divinity. If the body is addicted to sensuality, the soul becomes pleasure loving. To act like Hanuman is to try and transform the soul through acts of the body. Gopal knows this instinctively. He is making his body like that of a monkey to acquire the bhava of Rama's greatest devotee.'

'People will not tolerate such happenings in Galta much longer, elder brother,' Vishnu Das said. 'They are still talking about Charan Das—and now this! Do not say later that you were not warned.'

'Then, one day, near the end of summer, I felt Rama's presence achingly near me as Lord Hanuman must have done many aeons ago,' Gopal said, years later, describing to his disciples the moment when he acquired the bhava of Hanuman. 'The moment still stands out sharp in my memory, although the memory is not mine alone but one that I share with the great Hanuman: in that particular moment, "I" and "mine" were also "he" and "his".

'The sun is blazing down on the domed skulls of the hills surrounding Galta, ravaging the already gaunt rocks. A family of monkeys is scampering up a wasted *kikar* tree near the entrance, sending a clumsy crow flapping away. The afternoon is unbearably hot, mad and white from the sky down to the marbled courtyard of the temple. I feel an unbearable urge to run, run straight to Lord Rama. I step out into the courtyard. I kneel in joy on the burning stone beneath the fiery sky. And all I feel, besides the joy, is such an intense gratefulness that I wish could live the rest of my life, and die, in this gratitude to God.'

For a few days afterwards, Gopal was in a state of light stupor, as if awakened from a deep sleep flooded with

dreams. He resumed his life at the monastery, slept again in
Madhavacharya's room, but often seemed distracted as he
went about his daily chores. Madhavacharya was the only
person he talked to and to whom he tried to explain his
recent experiences, but he found that he had no words for
this. All he could do was to express his torment that the
memory of being with the Lord was becoming vaguer with
each passing day. The older man listened, consoled, provided
some of the missing words and encouraged the boy to travel
further on the path, heedless of the disapproval of Vishnu
Das and the other ascetics.

'There is no reason why you should show restraint when
the Lord has lifted you above yourself,' he said.

Gopal attended the aartis and sometimes listened to the
kirtan but seemed restless and did not sing himself.
Madhavacharya, who now openly looked after him, let it be
known that the boy was not well. This was true. The unripe
berries and the rotting fruit picked up from the dust and
eaten exacted a heavy toll. For the rest of his life, Gopal
suffered from a chronic stomach ailment. He often had to
take a little opium after the evening meal as an antidote to the
flatulence and dysentery to which he had become prone.
Casual visitors were often disconcerted because on days
when the humour of wind was particularly strong in his
body, he frequently belched while discoursing on elevated
spiritual subjects. It was his habit at these times to draw out
the end of a belch into a long 'O-o-o-om!' The gravity and
unselfconsciousness with which this was done had the effect
of transporting the belch into the realm of the sacred rather
than reducing 'Om', the immanent sound of the universe, to

an accident of the body.

Gopal began his practice of madhura bhava by first adopting the external emblems of this spiritual mood in which the aspirant strives to recreate within himself the anxious longing, and love, of Sita for her husband. Here, Dhamani proved to be invaluable. Ever since the evening he had heard Gopal sing, Dhamani was enthralled by the boy. He visited the monastery more frequently and it was apparent that he sought the boy's proximity as much as he did of his friend. He did not speak to Gopal, except sometimes to shyly enquire if 'father' needed anything, but hung around him as much as he could, watching him with adoring eyes. Told of Gopal's wish to dress like a woman, Dhamani took great pleasure in bringing 'father' costly Benares saris, Rajasthani ghagras, short cholis and thin muslin odhnis or thicker silk wraps for the days when the weather turned cool with the onset of the rains. He even brought a wig of long hair, and gold bangles and necklaces studded with precious stones from his own workshop, delighted at the joy these feminine accoutrements gave 'father'.

Gopal dressed as a woman for the next six months. People were astonished—and in the monastery, scandalized—by the change that took place in Gopal's comportment within the first couple of weeks. With each passing day he talked, behaved and moved more and more like a woman. Not self-consciously but instinctively, even to the extent of stepping out with left foot first and swaying his hips when he walked. In the temple courtyards and gardens, he gravitated toward groups of women, without arousing the least suspicion that he was not one of them. He bathed in the women's tank, but long before sunrise, before any of the monks had come down for a bath. At Dhamani's urging and with Madhavacharya's permission, he visited the jeweller's house in Johri Bazaar where, dressed as a woman, he insisted on spending his time with the women of the family in the inner apartments. The women were hesitant at first and needed to be reassured by Dhamani, but were soon charmed by his feminine deportment and temperament, so sympathetically attuned to their own, and treated him as one of their own. Like them he veiled his face whenever a strange male was near by. He helped out in the kitchen and took special pleasure in dressing Dhamani's twelve-year-old daughter after her bath and then combing and braiding her hair in two long plaits.

For six months Gopal cultivated the spiritual mood of Sita, his days spent in eager prayer and anxious longing for a vision of Rama. This mood deepened as days succeeded each other and the rainy season gave way to winter. He now had the feeling that his prayer never ceased. It continued night and day, its mood of pining for the beloved infiltrating even his dreams. Soon, the prayer expressed itself solely through a copious shedding of tears till the ducts ran dry. He stopped paying attention to food, sleep and other bodily concerns and was often seen sobbing piteously in one of the three Rama temples on the complex or in the monastery's cloistered garden. Many of the ascetics were moved by the extreme anguish of his heart but could offer no solace.

Madhavacharya had given strict instructions that Gopal's prayer was not to be interfered with, no matter what the provocation or the extreme manifestation it appeared to take. The prohibition was especially hard on Dhamani who wanted to rush forward to help whenever he saw 'father' collapse in a heap on the temple floor, the body motionless, as if unconscious, its joints loosened, almost dislocated.

Many years were to pass before Gopal was able to recount the experience coherently. 'One day I was in the garden in a small grove of mango trees. It was approaching sunset. I was alone. Except for the occasional bird cry and the sound of wings beating in the hushed air, it was unusually quiet. A few openings between the trees were letting in patches of roseate light as the sun disappeared below the horizon. I was sitting on the ground, in a hollow cavern of cool shadow, my back against a tree trunk, when I saw an incomparably beautiful woman appear at the edge of the grove. Her figure was bathed in a light so strong that for a moment I thought that part of the garden was on fire. Although the rest of the garden, the trees, the winter flowers, the springy grass and even the hills of Galta were all within my vision, the woman's form concealed all that was behind her. I knew the figure was of a woman, not a goddess. The expression on her face was extraordinarily moving, manifesting love, sorrow, compassion and endurance all at once. I wondered who she might be when I saw a large monkey, much bigger than any we had at Galta, drop from a branch and fall prostrate at her feet. A voice in my mind said, "Sita! Sita, daughter of king Janaka, wife of Lord Rama!" I stood up and repeatedly crying "Mother! Mother!" wanted to fling myself at her feet when she quickly moved toward me and entered my body. Overwhelmed with joy and wonder, I lost all consciousness and fell down.

'With this vision, my transformation into a woman—into Sita—during the periods of exquisitely heightened consciousness that now often overcame me, was complete. I menstruated the next morning and then again after a month.'

Here it must be said that although most of the disciples listened to this account of the vision and the young Gopal's subsequent transformation with awe, there were a few, Vivek among them, who struggled with their doubt over whether a man's physiology could indeed be changed to the extent that he could menstruate. They did not doubt their guru's truthfulness, of course, but wondered if it was the presence of blood in the faeces, a consequence of his stomach ailment that sometimes led to dysentery, which he had confused with menstrual discharge. Divining their unease, he addressed them with a smile,

'Yes, I know you have studied science in college and find it hard to believe what I have just related. But do not throw away our own traditions even as you absorb the knowledge of white men. The Vedanta has taught us that it is the mind of man that has created his body in its present form. Functioning at the behest of intense desire, it is the mind that is transforming the body every moment of life by decomposing and recomposing its physical elements. We do not really comprehend the full extent of the mind's mastery over the body. If your mind were to concentrate solely on one object, become one-pointed, you will be astonished by its extraordinary powers . . . also over your body.'

After this experience, which he only revealed to Madhavacharya at the time, Gopal began to pay special attention to his appearance. He asked Dhamani to get him an imported lipstick with which to colour his lips, and a bottle of Afghan snow cream that modern, well-off women used to make their skin fair and smooth. He rimmed his eyes with kohl and put fresh flowers in his wig every morning. When he was in a temple, his mood varied rapidly. To the consternation of the priest and the shocked disapproval of the devotees, he would step into the inner sanctum and affectionately caress Rama's idol, pat its cheek or chuck it under the chin. He would put the palm of his hand near the nostrils and feel the god was actually breathing. He sang, laughed, joked and conversed with the stone idol, sometimes catching hold of its hands and dancing. At other times, he would fall down at Rama's feet, grabbing them and sobbing convulsively as if his heart would break.

On the morning of 18 January 1947, the year India became free of British colonial rule, Gopal was sitting alone, as he often did, under the solemn arches of the mango trees in the monastery garden. There were heavy, dark clouds in the sky. The air was cold and limpid, with but a hint of the sun, the weak shafts of light on the leaves unable to undo the darkness in the grove. Then, suddenly, the wind picked up. It grew fierce and loud, ripping out the brittle branches and flinging them in confusion on the ground. Although the rain stayed in its cloud, it grew darker. Gopal was sitting with his eyes closed, not praying, not meditating, his senses vibrantly alive and his eyelids feeling every perturbation of light, when Lord

Rama finally blessed him with His *darshan*.

'I saw Him clearly with the eyes of the soul,' he was to recall to his disciples. 'Far more clearly than I would have ever seen him with the eyes of the body. At that time I did not know one could see things with eyes other than those of the body. The resplendence of his face and form impressed themselves so deeply on my memory that even now, almost twenty years later, it is still as if I see Him before me.

'I felt my jubilant heart lift up with the flap of a heron's wings into another world. My spirit was gambolling in its own interior landscape, an incomparably beautiful garden. And then I heard Him whisper tenderly in my soul, "Sita! My wife, my love!" I heard these words distinctly, I tell you, spoken inside me, addressed to the ears of my soul. They could not be confused with any other speech, so different in character from the words one hears in a silent conversation with one's self. Lord Rama had lit a fire of love in me and my soul no longer knew what it should do—whether it should speak or be silent, laugh or cry. All the senses, all thoughts had ceased. The silence was so vast and all-pervasive, you could hear it. The passion I felt for Him was so intense that I was like parchment stretched so tight it would split, and the rapture was so extreme that my body and soul actually wished to be torn to pieces, to die in this paradise of bliss. Ah, what a blessed death that gives such life!

'When I came back to the world, tears were flowing down my cheeks. They were no longer the tears of separation, of anxious longing, but a gift marked by profound peace. My soul found itself bathed in these tears of union without having felt them or knowing when and how it shed them.'

In the last six months, there had been a distinct change in Madhavacharya's relationship with Gopal. He was no longer the mentor although Gopal seemed oblivious to the old monk's abdication. Alone with Madhavacharya in his cell at night, Gopal would pour his heart out to the older man as he narrated his experiences, struggling to give expression to the bewildering states of his soul that fluctuated with such rapidity.

'When the Lord is with me, His presence palpable, it is as if I am a small child nestling in my mother's arms. Time and time again, my eyes open and I savour the joy of being in the haven of her tenderness but then fall asleep again in a slumber of intoxication. But such a state lasts only for a few hours, at the most for a couple of days, before I awaken into a world she has deserted. I feel dull and lethargic at first, and it takes a long time before my consciousness begins to function in a more than incomplete fashion. Then, as the memory of Rama's presence recedes, acute distress sets in. My anguish mounts, overwhelming my consciousness, just as joy once did.'

With his vast knowledge of Vaishnava mysticism, Madhavacharya tried to help Gopal make sense of his experiences. Comparing them to what was recorded in the texts on the lives of saints, he reassured the young man that his visions, whether seen through the eyes of the body or of the soul, and the ecstatic states accompanying them, were no different from theirs. Gopal's frequent loss of consciousness, the catching of breath in the throat, the disappearance of volition so that he was unable to move a finger except with great pain, were all signs of absorption in the Divine. And if he sometimes shivered with cold in such a state, then it was because the soul was enjoying so much happiness with the Lord that it was as if it had abandoned the body altogether and forgotten to give it life.

One by one, he sought to remove Gopal's anxieties about his disconcerting bodily symptoms. It was well known that states of intense longing and anguish had brought the saints sleeplessness. Their bodies, too, broke out in red spots as if the pores were on the verge of oozing blood. And the burning sensation, which sometimes became so unbearable that Gopal had to keep his body immersed in the tank for two to three hours, with a wet towel wrapped around his head, also found mention in the texts. The best antidote, Madhavacharya advised, was to adorn the body with garlands of sweet-smelling flowers and to smear it with fragrant sandalwood paste. Gopal had only to tell Dhamani and he would bring him the flowers and fresh paste every day. And Gopal was not to feel any anxiety, the mahant said, over the inordinate hunger for food that sometimes accompanied, but more often followed, the end of an ecstatic state. Gopal had been bewildered by this. He could eat enough to satisfy the hunger of five full-grown men. Immediately after eating, he felt hungry again as if he had not eaten at all. At these times he could digest vast quantities of food without difficulty in spite of his weak stomach.

Madhavacharya could not openly instruct the kitchen to break the rules governing the kind and quantities of food served to the ascetics. What he did was to ask Dhamani to keep all kinds of snacks and sweets in the mahant's room to which Gopal could help himself whenever he felt the urge: roasted peanuts, parched rice, Dhamani's favorite kachoris, Alwar milk cake and other *mithai* from Lakshmi Mishthan Bhandar in Johri Bazaar.

'Ah, I'm so glad I am not suffering from a disease!' was how Gopal reacted to the mahant's explanations.

Madhavacharya's relationship with Gopal had changed in that he did not explain from the superior stance of a teacher but from that of a student whose knowledge of the spiritual life, as compared to Gopal's, was peripheral. The deference in his voice and behaviour was unmistakable. In public he was still the mahant and Gopal an aspiring ascetic of uncertain status, a young man at the edge of ascetic life. Only Madhavacharya knew that he was also at the edge of the Self, from where he often fell into God.

Dhamani was his only confidant.

'My friend,' he said to the jeweller, 'the signs of all the nineteen spiritual moods, the coexistence of which has been called mahabhava, are manifest in him. Do you realize how rare mahabhava is? In all these hundreds of years only two or perhaps three saints are reported to have been able to sustain the tremendous impact mahabhava has on the body. Most of us spend our entire lives in perfecting just one of the moods. But all nineteen? At the same time? Unbelievable!'

'We are blessed, Maharaj, that we have been called upon to take care of father,' Dhamani said.

'Sitaram, do you ever wonder about how the Lord selects someone to whom he reveals Himself . . . while thousands of other mortals seek Him all their lives but in vain?'

'I am an ignorant man, Maharaj,' Dhamani replied, unable to understand the sadness that he sensed in his friend's voice. 'All I know is that I should take care of my family, serve you holy men, never take advantage of the simple-hearted but only of those who are greedy, and then, perhaps, after some lives I too may receive Rama's grace.'

'If anything ever happened to me, I fear they will not let him live in peace, Sitaram,' Madhavacharya said.

'Do not worry,' the jeweller reassured him, 'I will always take care of father as if he were my own son.'

The monastery buzzed with rumours about late-night eating orgies in the mahant's room, rumours that Vishnu Das had inspired and stoked.

'God knows what else is going on there,' Vishnu Das hinted darkly to the senior monks.

The campaign for the removal of Madhavacharya as the mahant had come along nicely. Anonymous letters, expressing outrage at the state of affairs in Galta which was becoming 'a nest for transvestite and homosexual activity' had been received at the royal court. Vishnu Das was thus unpleasantly surprised at the treatment the delegation of three senior monks, with himself as the spokesman, received at the Jaipur durbar where they had gone to seek Sawai Man Singh's intervention in the monastery's affairs. The

Maharaja had refused to see them and a haughty young official had made them feel like naïve fools for presuming to seek Madhavacharya's removal.

'The Maharaja has only the power to appoint Galta's mahant, not to remove him,' the official had said. 'The provocation has to be extreme for the durbar to interfere in Galta's affairs, like at the time of the mahant Madhuracharya three hundred years ago when the monks were openly living with concubines. And the Maharaja's power was absolute then, as was the case with Sawai Jai Singh. Though even at *that* time, the mahant was not removed but only forced to carry out certain reforms. You have no evidence of anything being seriously wrong. If a couple of your people go a little crazy and start dressing in women's clothes, do you believe His Highness will seriously think of doing something about that? The British are leaving, the country will soon be independent. He has to worry about the future of Jaipur state, about what these Congress-walas are upto. He has no time to waste on such trivial matters.'

Vishnu Das held Madhavacharya responsible for this humiliation. His mounting anger combined with helplessness was producing a potent bile that was corroding his heart and his composure.

Talking to his disciples when he was much older and known as Ram Das Baba, Gopal remembered an extraordinary incident: 'Two nights after the Lord's darshan, when my soul was still lagging behind my senses which were returning to the world more quickly, something very strange happened. Madhavacharya had just placed Ram-lalla in his lap. I had lighted the lamp and was about to lie down when Ram-lalla climbed out of Madhavacharya's lap and followed me to my bed on the floor. At first I thought it was a fancy of mine. How could it be otherwise! Could Ram-lalla love me more than Madhavacharya who had been loving and serving Him tenderly for all these years?

'The next morning we did not talk about what had happened. The statue, too, lay lifeless in its usual place on the window sill next to the mahant's bed. But again at night, when I went to bed, Ram-lalla came tripping down. I actually saw—just as I see you before me—Ram-lalla stretching His little arms and entreating me to carry Him. And I did. Madhavacharya was crying.

'"Ram-lalla has shown Himself to me and has thus fulfilled my life's ambition," he said, tears rolling down his cheeks. "But He wants to stay with you now. I know he will be happy with you. His happiness is mine too. But it hurts so much to lose Him at the very moment of finding Him."

'And then I heard Madhavacharya weep, quietly at first and then with loud, wrenching sobs that emptied his heart of its sadness but began to choke his mind with a clogging despair.

'Ram-lalla has been with me ever since,' Ram Das said, pointing to the small statue made of eight metals which he always kept on the wooden stool next to his bed.

Chapter Ten

The kirtan, unbroken for over four hundred years, did not stop when the body was discovered a couple of hours before dawn. The two young monks went on singing:

He really lives who worships Rama
He really lives who adores Him

even as the monastery came awake to the sound of wooden sandals clattering on cobbled stone, and alarmed shouts of 'Mahantji is dead!' The song wavered but then braced itself as the singers regained their composure, resisting the urge to get up and rush out along with the others.

By the time the police arrived, well past noon, Madhavacharya's corpse had been fished out of the bathing tank, washed, wrapped in an uncut piece of white cotton cloth, and placed on the marble floor of the main puja hall. Most of the monks stood uncertainly around in small groups, the day's chores left undone, although Vishnu Das had insisted on conducting a hurried morning aarti. He stood to one side of the body, grim and authoritative, occasionally raising a forefinger to beckon one of the monks and whisper urgent instructions. Although yet to be formally installed as the new mahant of Galta, Vishnu Das had already taken over.

The inspector who conducted the interviews in the mahant's office thought Gopal looked considerably younger than his eighteen years. He liked the boy's open face, now frequently clouding over with sadness, but felt that he was not 'all there' in the head. Answering simple questions about his ancestral village and his parents and how he happened to be in Galta, Gopal's voice and the light in his eyes would sometimes just fade away and the inspector had to wait for their reanimation. As the last person to see the mahant alive, his testimony was crucial and the policeman was patient, taking care not to frighten the boy who stood in front of him like a deer poised for flight. No, Gopal had not heard the mahant go out after they went to bed. No, nothing unusual had happened last night. The mahant had followed his normal routine before going to sleep. He had taken the statue of Ram-lalla in his lap, sung to it for a while, and then fallen silent, his eyes closed in contemplation. Gopal had blown out the lamp and gone to sleep.

Gopal knew he had not been truthful. He had not mentioned Ram-lalla's desertion. That was a secret. The man questioning him was gentle, unlike the violent baton-wielding bullies all policemen were reputed to be. Yet, he would not understand. How could anyone!

After a week of cursory investigation, Madhavacharya's death was declared an accident. He had slipped and fallen into the deep end of the bathing tank for men where the water was almost fifty feet deep. No one knew for certain but it was presumed that like most monks, or indeed most inhabitants of this land-locked desert state, he could not swim. For a few months, there was a persistent rumour that the mahant of Galta had been murdered. There were whispers that he had been involved in sexual orgies with transvestites and that he had been strangled and thrown into the tank by a group of senior monks led by the present mahant, Vishnu Das. For most of Jaipur's citizens, though, the rumours were too bizarre to be given credence.

To his disciples Gopal would later say: 'But *I* know what happened. When Ram-lalla left him, his heart broke. He could not bear to live any longer. But see how strong his pride was—Madhavacharya would rather have died than live in surrender to His will.'

At Dhamani's insistence, Gopal left Galta the same afternoon to stay with the jeweller's family.

'Father,' Dhamani had said. 'With Vishnu Das as the new mahant, you cannot live here any longer. I shall put my carriage at your disposal. You can come back here whenever you want to worship the gods.'

A fierce wind was whipping up, summoning shiftless clouds to cover the sky, as they drove away in Dhamani's carriage. The trees lining the dirt road that cut through the jungle began to rock and then toss and plunge like wild horses. Sitting at the back, clutching the statue of Ram-lalla tightly in both hands as the carriage lurched and clattered over potholes and stones, Gopal looked back at the hills of

Galta without emotion. The temples were hidden from view by the thick vegetation but the monastery, higher up on the middle hill, was still visible. With Madhavacharya dead, he need never return. The gods—Rama, Sita, Hanuman—were in any case carried securely within his heart.

He woke up the next morning with a heavy feeling of lethargy. The lethargy increased throughout the day. By the evening he felt exhausted and Dhamani had to coax him to eat dinner. The food tasted like ash and he could barely swallow a mouthful of his favourite sweets that Dhamani pressed on him. During the next month, there were brief intervals of elation when he gorged himself on whatever was available—puris and kachoris left over from breakfast, last night's dal—and was then immediately racked by attacks of dysentery. But even the excruciating stomach pains were preferable to the long periods of depression in which he now found himself. Sometimes, for no reason at all, while sitting in the kitchen with the women, he had to thrust a fist into his mouth to keep from breaking out into loud sobs. Or he would flee to the bazaar to seek the press of other bodies in the crowds in order to stop himself from screaming. The world, whether inside the house or in the bazaars, was bereft of all colour and blurred and insubstantial, as if seen through a haze. The brilliant blue of Jaipur's winter sky seemed to be a perpetual dirty grey.

Dhamani showed concern; his family was more than solicitous. But Gopal felt indifferent to all of them, as if a scorching blast had raced through each pore of his body, wiping out all traces of affection. Even thoughts of his mother, which had always been accompanied by a surge of deep feeling, now left him cold. And as for Madhavacharya, it was as if his mentor whom he had loved next only to his mother had never existed.

The worst part of his condition was not the apathy but an unknown fear that clutched at his heart and made him so restless that he could not sit quietly in prayer for even fifteen minutes. The fear came rushing in whenever his mind moved toward stillness. He paced his room, unable either to sit or lie down. He stepped out into the veranda where he watched the craftsmen fashion gold ornaments but felt a compulsion to leave the moment his attention was engaged by the exercise of their skill. He wandered in and out of the women's apartments or went down to the ground floor where Dhamani presided over his shop but could never stop for long anywhere, his gaze unable to rest on an object or a scene for any length of time.

Dhamani worried as he watched 'father's' face become more haggard and pale every day, his eyebrows drawn together in a perpetual frown. The look in his eyes was desperate, belying his deliberate movements. Hearing him whimper at night, Dhamani moved his cot into his own room, next to the bed he shared with his wife, but nothing seemed to help Gopal's worsening condition. Taking the mornings off from his business, Dhamani took him around to Jaipur's many temples. This was 'father's' natural habitat and Dhamani hoped a re-immersion in the Divine would cure him of whatever was wrong. But Gopal could not bear to stay longer than a few minutes in any temple, and only minutes after entering a temple he would start tugging at the jeweller's sleeve in his impatience to leave.

One afternoon Dhamani thought he had almost identified the disease. They were sitting down for lunch, the tiny silver bowls on the thalis in front of them filled with Marwari delicacies—*sangri ka saag, dal-bati churma* and *bela*, the delicious balls of lentil flour fried in butter. The women had taken Gopal's loss of appetite as a challenge to their culinary skills and were trying hard to revive it. They were hovering around him even now, especially Dhamani's fourteen-year-old daughter who was coaxing him to eat, playfully trying to stuff a laddoo into his mouth. Suddenly, Gopal rushed out of the room. He returned a few minutes later, his face looking even more troubled than usual, his manner highly agitated. Standing in front of Dhamani, he asked in a piteous voice very close to tears,

'Can't you tell me what is the disease I have? I saw a white worm go out of my body with the urine.'

'It is all right, father. Every one has a lust-worm in his body. It produces evil thoughts and prompts evil actions. The lust-worm has now left your body. You need not worry.'

Dhamani's wife shared his opinion when they discussed the incident in the evening.

'He is the purest of men, but a man nevertheless, with the body of a young male,' she said. 'It is the virility backing up in his system that makes him sick. He needs to be with a woman.'

'You are right, Paro's mother,' Dhamani said. 'The only cure for this disease is for him to sleep with a woman.'

The same evening, on their way to one of the more expensive brothels in Tripolia bazaar, frequented by Jaipur's minor nobility and richer merchants, Dhamani had tried his best to prepare 'father' for what awaited him. He was not sure, though, if he had succeeded. 'Father's' heart was much too pure, his mind still cocooned in the innocence of childhood. He had clung to Dhamani's arm, refusing to enter the room alone where three attractive young prostitutes, none of them older than eighteen, were waiting. When one of the girls caught hold of his hand and laughingly tried to pull him inside, Gopal began to cry. He fell down on his knees and joining his hands in prayer began calling the prostitutes 'Mother Sita!', 'Mother Kali!' The girls were laughing now and piled onto him, trying to pull off his clothes. One of them even brushed the knuckles of her hand against his genitals. At this last touch, he fainted. The prostitutes, suddenly sober now, called Dhamani. They tried to revive Gopal by fanning his face and wetting his forehead with the edge of a saree soaked in rose-scented water. While one of the girls was rearranging Gopal's cotton shift, Dhamani was amazed to see that 'father's' genitals had contracted and retreated into his body like the limbs of a tortoise.

As they stepped down from the bus on the Delhi-Jaipur highway, Dhamani groaned. He did not relish the prospect of a five-mile walk on a dusty, unpaved road even if it was winter and the midday sun was not as hot in the countryside as in the city.

'Let us wait and see if an ox cart comes along, father,' he said, trying to restrain Gopal's eagerness to set off at once.

The visit to the brothel had had consequences. Gopal's

restlessness had definitely abated and the anxious expression on his face was no longer quite so pronounced. Instead, he was now given to uncontrollable bouts of weeping which could overtake him at any time of the day or night. In such a state he could do nothing except cry out 'Mother! Mother!!' His plaintive calls were addressed to the Goddess Sita, of course, imploring her presence, but they suggested to Dhamani that it might help if 'father' was taken to Deogarh to spend some time with his earthly mother. And, indeed, for the first time in three months since leaving Galta, Gopal seemed cheerful. He was almost skipping along the narrow mud embankment winding through the tawny fields in which the wheat was standing tall, ready to be harvested. His restlessness no longer sprang from fear but from hope.

'Walk faster. We are almost there,' he urged the portly jeweller along.

Dhamani was sweaty and hungry, his stomach rumbling with the swish of wind pressing down for blessed release. He was glad, though, that he had brought 'father' home.

Amba had had little sleep ever since she asked the astrologer to read out Dhamani's postcard from Jaipur. Her Gopal was coming home. After three years! How she had longed to see her son during those years, but the sadhu's prohibition on visiting him at the monastery had left her helpless. The pain of being separated from her child had been terrible, and now that he was returning, she ached to hold him to her heart.

But when Gopal finally arrived, she barely had time to gather him in her embrace before curious women came tumbling out of the neighbouring houses. Jaipur was not far

and Galta was a famous pilgrimage centre. They had heard
that the boy had become insane, that he dressed like a
woman and cried 'Ram, Ram!' all the time, that he was
behaving like a monkey, jumping from branch to branch. To
their disappointment, Gopal seemed normal enough, polite,
gentle and agreeable. His manner did not appear to have
changed.

'You still sing, son?' one of the women asked.

'Yes, mother,' he said.

His voice was a little deeper but still sweet and oddly
thrilling. His shoulders had broadened, drawing attention
away from the swell to his hips. He had remained slim,
though, and the breasts were no longer so pronounced. His
face was soft but haggard, with the shadow of a beard.

By the evening, they had all come—the devout Sundari,
the widowed sister of the astrologer, the women from the
Brahmin and Rajput households where he had sung as a boy.
They stayed till late that night, and returned early the next
morning, and the next. When they asked him whether he had
come back to Deogarh for good, to settle down and look
after his old mother, Gopal only smiled. His behaviour was
amiable enough, but some of the women, and certainly his
mother, sensed his detachment from everything that
belonged to the world they knew and lived in. Soon he began
spending much of his day at the cremation ground at the foot
of the hill, praying and meditating (at least his eyes were
closed all the time, observers reported) and was liable to get
annoyed if disturbed. He did not climb up even once to the
rest house or the Vishnu temple.

Although Gopal's health improved and he ate his meals

with evident relish, Amba was alarmed by his uninterrupted inwardness and his complete indifference to all the small details of her life and the affairs of the village. She told him of the tension between the Rajputs and the Jats which was again mounting as Independence approached. With the expected waning of the durbar's influence, people felt that the question of which was the dominant community here, in Deogarh, was bound to be reopened. She gave him news of her own family, of how her brothers had visited her last winter but had not offered any monetary help. Times were hard and although there was sufficient money coming in as rent from the fields, a large sum would be certainly needed for his marriage. Gopal heard her patiently but she was not sure if he was actually listening. It was apparent that he was often distracted and the animation he sometimes showed was perhaps because he was responding to her voice, not to her words. Amba feared a relapse if her son's connection to the world continued to remain tenuous.

Since Gopal had not reacted to the broad hint she had thrown about his marriage, Amba took the silence as his acquiscence to her plans. There was no better cure than marriage for the maladies that afflicted the young, nothing that brought them back to earth from their fanciful flights as did the task of setting up a family. Amba already had her eye on the astrologer's sixteen-year-old niece. The girl was no beauty, she had the solid build of Jat women rather than a Brahmin delicacy of form. But she was a willing worker with a strong back and wide hips who would work hard in the household and bear healthy sons. It was all to the good that she was an orphan, a burden on her uncle and aunt who were therefore less likely to raise objections to the match because of the rumours about her son not being quite right in the head. The horoscopes were studied by the girl's uncle who was quick to find no heavenly impediments to the match. At Amba's urging, the astrologer also found an auspicious day for the nupitals that very winter, in three weeks time.

They were sitting outside the hut with Dhamani, drinking tea, when Amba told Gopal about the marriage arrangements.

'Marriage? Mine? Mother, what are you saying!'

He then turned to Dhamani.

'Only you can explain to her why I can never marry, how I can never be a householder.'

'Perhaps my mother's proposal was necessary for me to give up the last traces of my worldliness, sweep away the remaining gossamer threads of past attachments and those that were being spun for me in the future,' Ram Das explained to his disciples. 'She made me realize that I was like Kartikeya who came home one day and saw a scratch mark on his mother's cheek, the goddess Parvati.

'"How did you get that ugly mark on your cheek, mother?" he asked.

'"Don't you remember? You scratched a cat this morning."

'"Yes, I did, but how come the mark is on your cheek?"

'"That is because I am the essence of all that is female in the universe," the Divine mother replied.

'Kartikeya was astonished to hear this and decided never to marry. Whom could he marry? Every woman was his mother. That is also true of me.'

Although he was still apprehensive, his mind not yet quite free of fear, Gopal now knew what he must do. He did not want to live in Deogarh, but also not in the city, he said to Dhamani when he accompanied him to the bus stop that afternoon. What he wanted was to stay in a place where he could be alone with God, to pray and worship, to try and recover what he may have lost.

'I was going to suggest something like that myself, father,' Dhamani said. 'I have this property near the Purana Ghat. An old garden, lying in ruins. My wife wants me to build a summer house there, like that of the Golchas. What do I need a summer house for, I tell her. Is a summer house the boat that will take me to the other shore? Live there, father. I will build a temple for you. Spend your days and nights with Sita and Rama. Be with God.'

It was arranged that the jeweller would return as soon as the garden was ready for habitation and take Gopal back to Jaipur.

Chapter Eleven

The garden was large but unkempt. It was about
two-thirds the size of the neighbouring Vidiadhar garden,
named after the architect who had given reality to Maharaja
Jai Singh's dream to build a new capital city after the models
of the German towns of Bayreuth and Erlangen. A small
pavilion, now in ruins, stood in the centre. Weeds grew out of
the cracks between the stones in the walls. A marble
fountain, yellow and veined with age, lay broken in two
pieces in front of the pavilion, the water channel half filled
with mud and stones that had come loose from its sides. The
fruit-bearing trees needing care—mango and guava—were
long gone. Only the hardy survivors remained—a few
tamarind and neem trees.

Gopal had moved into the simple one-room hut with a
thatched roof and a brick outhouse that stood next to the
well in one corner of the garden. The well had been cleaned
and was equipped with a shiny new cast iron pulley, a brass
bucket and a thick rope. Twice a day, one of Dhamani's
servants, a mildly retarded boy a few years younger than
Gopal, came with cooked food from the house. He filled the
pitcher with water, washed one of Gopal's two shifts, and

swept the floor. Dhamani came three to four afternoons in the week, not to talk but only to be in 'father's' presence. 'Father' had replaced Madhavacharya and the hut had replaced Galta as the site of his recurrent pilgrimage.

Living by himself in Dhamani's garden, absorbed in prayer and contemplation, his days and nights merging into each other, their boundaries blurred, Gopal began to recognize himself less and less with each passing day. At times he would laugh, hum or talk to himself, wholly engrossed in his inner theatre. At others, he would be restless and anxious, pace in front of the hut, rise from his favourite seat under the tamarind tree next to the well only to sit down there again. He no longer resisted his impulses to dance, jump about and scream even when the servant boy was present. Sometimes, he felt cool and light, floating above the ground as he walked. On other days his body felt heated up as at the height of summer, and then his head was heavy and each cell of his body groaned. The beauty of the leaves on the tamarind tree gently riding the waves of a breeze could hold his attention for hours.. At other times, his eyes would dart about, his glance returning terrified from wherever it sought to linger. He heard strange noises from afar: the long-drawn notes of an exquisitely played flute but also terrifying screams. Many of his bodily rhythms that he took for granted became unpredictable. Sometimes, after exhalation the breath was held outside, and after inhalation inside, till he was at the point of choking before his breathing would suddenly resume its normal rhythm. Once, he put a finger in his right eye, and found that it had lost the power to blink. He did not know how long he sat there, unblinking. He was thoroughly frightened.

'O Lord!' he cried out silently, 'Is this the result of calling on Thee? Is the medicine that I need worsening the disease? Look at the terrible afflictions my surrender has brought upon this body . . . But it does not matter. Let the body become sick. Let it go. But do not forsake me. Reveal yourself again, Lord. I have no other refuge.'

He wept for a while and then his mind was filled with a fierce happiness, but only for a while, and then it sank back into a familiar state of gnawing discontent.

At first he thought it was an apparition produced by his mind, for he had begun to mistrust his eyes, as he did his ears. What he saw from a distance was a tall, well-built sadhu, naked except for a thin strip of cloth carelessly flapping around the genitals, enter the garden through the gate to the Agra road.

'Who is that?' he asked the servant boy, more to confirm the evidence of his eyes than for information.

'A holy man, brother.'

'Bring him here.'

He did not know what so moved him but he began to cry when the middle-aged sadhu, his years belied only by the grey hair on his chest, stood before him. Even as he wept, there was a mounting feeling of lightness in his heart, as if a heavy burden was being lifted from it. The sadhu sat down. His soft brown eyes were grave but kind.

'Tell me, son,' he said, without the exchange of a single preliminary.

Like a child prattling about his experiences in a world he did not quite fathom, Gopal poured out his fears: his strange visions, the peculiar changes in the body, the dread of madness.

'Why are all these things happening to me? Why do I lose control over my senses? Have I become mad for calling on the Lord with all my heart?'

'You are not mad, son, but in a fluctuating state of mahabhava. Yours is a divine gift, a stream of grace, but one which needs to be channelled through discipline lest it destroy your body and your mind.'

'Will you teach me? Will you accept me as your disciple?'

'We shall see,' the sadhu said, his smile promising more than his words.

Nangta, 'the Naked One', as Gopal came to think of his guru since most of the time he disdained to wear even his abbreviated loincloth, lived in the garden for eighteen months. He had expected only to stay for a few hours. On his way from the banks of the Narmada to the Badrinath temple in the remote fastness of the Himalayas, Nangta had broken his journey at Galta. There, he heard the story about Madhavacharya and the boy whom the late mahant had one day brought back with him from the Balaji temple in Mehndipur. He had politely listened to the toothless old monk, dressed in a woman's long, crimson skirt, prattle on about the boy's amazing visions and Madhavacharya's conviction that he was a born Paramahamsa, soon destined to realize his true nature. Nangta was sceptical but intrigued enough to mention the conversation to the new mahant when they were strolling together in the monastery's garden after the evening service.

'Ah, my friend,' Vishnu Das said. 'Who should know better than you how hard it is to travel on the path of the spirit! Even a reasonable hope of reaching the goal requires years of arduous training and discipline. How long did it take you? Thirty years? Twenty-five? There are no untutored mystical geniuses around any more, my friend. Our monks are both lazy and credulous. Their wish is for sudden transformations. They long for metamorphoses that they believe await them just around the corner.'

'Hmm-m,' Nangta hesitated with his agreement. 'But could Madhavacharya be so completely wrong in his judgement?'

'I am told the boy lives in a garden outside Jaipur and that he is even more mentally unbalanced than when he was here,' Vishnu Das said, his manner perceptibly colder. 'If you are interested you could go and see for yourself. The garden is on the way to the railway station.'

When Nangta walked up to the boy that morning, he was immediately struck by the hopelessness on his face. It was clear from his pleading eyes that he was at the edge of madness, that he was making a last desperate effort to fight the chaos that raged within him. Yet, looking beyond the apparent, Nangta saw in Gopal all the bodily signs of an extraordinary spiritual potential. He was that rarest of gems from which Nangta could not walk away before doing his bit to polish it to its full brilliance.

At the very beginning, Nangta explained to Gopal the need to practice spiritual discipline. It was essential for an aspirant to follow the path and procedures prescribed by the scriptures, so as to secure the conviction that his visions and experiences were not deceptions produced by the mind but absolutely real, since they had been experienced by many others who had followed the same path. Relieved of all doubt and fear, the aspirant could then proceed untroubled toward the ultimate goal. For Nangta, the ultimate goal was nirvikapla samadhi, the direct experience, without images or symbols, not of things heavenly and divine but of a universal consciousness in which there is neither 'I' nor 'You', a state entailing the obliteration of thought and the destruction of language. Beyond having faith in the existence of a higher power, Nangta did not believe there was a need for worship of deities and ritual practices. All that was necessary was personal effort, through self-control and meditation, although he allowed that the human mind, at least at the initial state, needed visual and aural supports to help it concentrate and establish itself in meditation.

On the full moon day of July 1950, the day of the guru in Nangta's monastic tradition, Gopal was initiated as the Naked One's disciple. He had fasted the whole day, as had Nangta. A festive meal, prepared by the women in Dhamani's household, awaited them after the initiation was over. At first, Dhamani was unhappy with the idea of Nangta staying in his garden. But essentially a good man constantly seeking to be better, he soon realized that the real reason for his resentment was this unexpected intrusion into his intimacy with 'father'. At this stage of his journey, Gopal needed the sadhu, Dhamani told himself, and he himself should be content to serve rather than want to possess. And so the jeweller, a humble man inspite of his great wealth, felt grateful for the chance to gather merit as the person who would serve the newly initiated sadhu his first meal.

The abbreviated ceremony, with just Gopal and Nangta as participants, began at midnight. It took place out in the open, next to the well where a sacrificial fire had been lit. Nangta had Gopal sit on the other side of the fire, a brass plate heaped with white and black sesame seeds between them. Nangta then began to chant the sacred mantras which the prospective disciple repeated after him. At the end of each mantra, the guru and disciple would pick up a handful of sesame seeds and throw them into the fire. The sun was beseeched for intellectual clarity, but, above all, the mantras were vows of renunciation and prayers for the purification of the sense organs.

'A reflection of Consciousness, I, who am the nature of God Himself, offer to the fire all my desires—for wife, son, wealth, honour, beauty, and all other objects. I renounce them all!'

'I am now beyond life and death, hunger and grief, satisfaction and dissatisfaction.'

The monsoon clouds were racing across the moon when Nangta cut off Gopal's topknot in the flickering light and consigned it to the flames as a final gift to the fire. Gopal was then asked to take off his shift and walk naked seven times around a small pyre of wood before lying down on top of it. His funeral rites were performed, symbolic of his farewell to

a worldly past and birth into a spiritual future, and then the
pyre was lit with burning coal from the sacrificial fire. Gopal
was dead when he stood up, though his body was still alive.
Henceforth, whenever he said 'I', the pronoun would mean
the Brahman, the cosmic spirit, not the body or mind of a
youth who had been called Gopal. Nangta then whispered
the mantra of his own monastic tradition in Gopal's left ear.
This mantra would henceforth guide the disciple's
meditation. It would determine if the meditation would be
devotional, impersonal or ecstatic in nature and over the
course of time would channel Gopal's own nature in the
same direction. Once he became an adept, the mantra would
allow him to switch on at will the bliss that he had
involuntarily experienced in the garden of Galta's
monastery. Nangta then explained the proper way to sit in
meditation, how to breathe, how to relax the mind and how
to harness it with the use of the mantra. The guru then bowed
before the disciple, spoke out his new ascetic name: Ram
Das. And then the ceremony was over.

'I am your guru now,' Nangta said, bringing his face
close to Gopal's and looking deep into his eyes, 'your Rama
and Sita, your Krishna and Radha, your Shiva and Shakti. I
am your mantra and I am your tantra. Wherever you will
ever want to go, all paths will lead through me. Always
remember that worship of the guru includes the worship of
all deities. Meditating on the guru is to meditate on all the
gods. To repeat the guru's name is like chanting the seventy
million sacred mantras.'

There was no hesitation, not the slightest fear, as Gopal
surrendered to a stream of love which began to flow through

channels that had long run dry. He fell at Nangta's feet, bathing them in joyful tears.

When the servant came next morning with the midday meal, Nangta flung the thalis to the ground.

'What is all this vegetarian stuff you bring us every day?' he shouted. 'Grass for cattle! I want meat!'

'Meat is never cooked in our house, Maharaj,' the frightened boy replied.

'Then tell that fat Dhamani to buy a pound of mutton. Muslim butchers have the best cuts. Bring oil, cooking utensils, onions, garlic and spices. I shall cook and feed my disciple tonight.'

A strict vegetarian since birth, brought up in a Brahmin household where even onions and garlic were looked upon as disgustingly impure, Gopal was ordered to chop and wash the bloody pieces of goat meat while Nangta watched him closely for any sign of disgust. When he had cooked the meat, Nangta served the curry to Gopal in a bowl he always carried with him and which Gopal had thought was made of old ivory. It was the top half of a human skull.

'Eat!' Nangta commanded.

Dutifully, Gopal began to chew on a piece of meat. It gave off a loathsome stench and was of a stringy texture that he had never associated with food. To judge from Nangta's vigorous mastication, it was also undercooked. Gopal could not swallow and gagged each time he tried.

'Eat,' Nangta said, more gently. 'This is your guru's *prasad*, higher than the offering sanctified by all the gods together.'

Gopal looked at Nangta. He saw his guru's form clothed

in beauty, his skin shining with a bronze sheen. He saw his sleekly muscled body, the thick penis, shades darker than the surrounding nut-brown skin, resting against the thigh. He saw the eyes glow in his guru's bearded face and the ripple of a muscle in his throat. Then he found himself eating. Nangta made no comment.

The next day Nangta disappeared early in the morning, returning only around noon. He brought with him a small piece of rotting flesh which was staining the sheet of newspaper in which it was wrapped rust brown. This was human flesh, he announced. He did not offer an explanation.

'Touch it with your tongue,' he commanded, holding it in front of Gopal's mouth.

The stench was overpowering, and Gopal found himself retching. Nangta waited till the spasm subsided and Gopal had wiped away the involuntary tears.

'Can it be done?' Gopal asked, keeping his eyes averted from the grey-brown mass.

'There is nothing to it, child,' he said. 'Just look.'

He bit off a portion with his strong white teeth, chewed on it and then extended his hand to offer the rest to Gopal. Gopal concentrated on his guru's face, rediscovering its fascination. He felt an upsurge of love irrigate the smallest pores of his body. A well-known happiness began to irradiate from the centre of his heart, lighting up the darkest corners of his mind. All he saw was his guru's pearly teeth and his beautiful tapering fingers as he took the raw flesh from his hands and bit into it.

'It really was human flesh, you know,' Nangta laughed, and Gopal with him.

'You know the enemy now,' Nangta said, suddenly serious. 'Renouncing is not a matter of intent or will. It is the body which finds it so difficult to give up—aversion more than pleasure, repulsion more than desire.'

Nangta was astonished. In his thirty years of wanderings as a sadhu that took him from his village near Simla to the remotest corners of the land, he had never met anyone with Gopal's gift for spiritual life. Normally, Nangta would have first instructed a beginner in meditation to sit on a cushion since his legs might ache if he sat cross-legged on a hard seat, his untrained mind thus diverted to the travails of the body than to thoughts of God. Afterwards, as the student progressed, the seat would become harder till finally the student could meditate while sitting on bare ground without being distracted. Similarly, the period of meditation would have been only gradually increased. Gopal did not need an incremental approach. From the very beginning, he could meditate for hours sitting on bare ground. But meditation was not even remotely a matter of its mechanics. Nangta waited for a few weeks, waiting for the guru bhava to take firm hold of Gopal's mind before initiating him into the discipline of guru meditation. The guru bhava, too, came easily to Gopal. He had lived so long in the madhura bhava that it had become a natural state of his mind, its emotional habitat. Transferring this mood from God to guru was as easy as an infant moving from one breast of the mother to another, a brief moment of disorientation before the resumption of bliss.

Gopal ate Nangta's leftovers, drank the water with which he washed his hands and feet, picked up the dust from places where he rested and smeared it all over his own body. He constantly sought the Naked One's proximity and raptly gazed at his guru while the guru ate, slept or meditated. He was like a painter familiarizing himself with every singularity of his subject's face so as to capture its essential expression that transcends all detail. Soon, he could visualize his guru's face and form, keeping them steady, unchanging, even when his eyes were closed. In contrast to the painter, though, Gopal's adoration took him beyond a purely observational stance. His own face began to eerily mirror the guru's characteristic expression when in repose: eyes half closed, lips pressed firmly together, the head gently moving forward and backward. When he walked, his strides were longer and more confident, like those of his beloved Nangta. He was fully aware of the deep changes in his body-mind entity: short periods of a kind of double identity when he alternated with Nangta, when it was the guru who stood up but the disciple who sat down. In these extremely pleasant fugue-like states, the dissolution of the boundary that separated him from the guru did not evoke dread but a kind of intoxication in which he would cry out, 'Nangta and I are one. I am Nangta!'

Before the start of the actual meditation, Gopal carried out a fast based on the phases of the moon. On the full moon night of that month, he ate thirteen handfuls of rice, each consecrated by the touch of Nangta's tongue. This amount was diminished by a handful each night of the waning half of the lunar month. On the day preceding the new moon when he began the meditation after midnight, he did not eat at all.

The garden was as still as the night sky. Neither a leaf nor a star was stirring. Gopal sat under the tamarind tree, unmoving and erect, breathing slowly and rhythmically till his breath slowed down so much as to be barely perceptible. The object of his meditation was Nangta.

'My guru is in my head. He is in my forehead. My beloved Nangta is in my ears. He is the light of my eyes. He has come into my throat. He is in my arms, in my hands, in each of my fingers. He is now in my heart, now spreading through my veins, entering each cell. Nangta is in my abdomen. He is in my back, in my thighs, in my genitals. He is in my knees. He is in my legs, in my feet.'

Thus Gopal installed Nangta in his body, limb by limb, while silently repeating 'Guru Om, Guru Om.' The installation took three hours and was accompanied by a sensation of lightness and deep joy. Fully absorbed in the meditation now, Gopal had the feeling the guru was everywhere—in the mantra, in the branches and leaves of the tamarind tree, in the ground on which he sat, in the bejewelled canopy of the sky above him. The mantra itself was like a running refrain in the background, like the drone of a tanpura of which he was no longer consciously aware. As the meditation deepened, he felt a stab of pain at the base of the spine, as if a blunt wooden spike had been tamped against the coccyx with the single blow of a hammer. The pain was followed by an extraordinarily pleasing sensation flashing upward through the spine like a reversed bolt of lightning. Suddenly, with the roar of a waterfall, he felt a stream of liquid light enter his brain and fill the cranium. The roaring became louder and the light brighter, pouring into his head like moonlight through a window, flooding the glass without altering it. Gopal felt himself slipping out of his body, encircled by a halo of light which was not only a visual perception but also an exquisite sensation. Indeed, his body appeared to recede, become a mere dot in the distance. Gopal was now pure consciousness, a sea of light, unaffected by feeling or sensation. He was without an outline, spreading in all directions without any barriers or obstructions, existing in every point of space.

The state of exaltation accompanying this reversal—of no longer being a small point of awareness that existed in the confines of a body but a vast circle of consciousness in which the body was but a tiny dot—was indescribable. After a while—the duration of this 'while' equally impossible to pin down—the circle began to narrow. Gopal felt himself contracting. He became smaller and smaller. The outline of his body, starting with the head and then extending to the torso and its extremities, began to take shape and dimly intrude upon his consciousness. It was followed by a perception of its mass and density, and of the beat of his heart, as his corporeality reconstituted itself. He became aware of the silence in the garden, felt a prickling sensation spread through his arms and legs as they stirred to life. With an effort he opened his eyes, prising open the lids that seemed gummed together.

Dawn was imminent. Gopal continued to sit where he was, unable to move, listening to the darkness dissolve around him. He watched the trees in the garden, the hut, the broken marble fountain and the pavilion come alive with the morning light and regain substance, no longer shadows of themselves. With another effort of will he raised his arms that still felt limp and unlocked his stiff legs. He massaged his thighs and the soles of his feet to restore the circulation in his legs before he could stand up and hobble towards the hut, still a little dazed. The hut was empty. Nangta's reed mat was neatly folded and rolled up against a wall. Gopal lay down in the spot where Nangta always slept, drawing out the warm impression of his guru's body from the hard mud floor, wrapping it around him like a sheet as he fell into a deep sleep.

It was close to midnight when he awoke. He had slept straight through for fifteen hours. Nangta had not returned. Gopal was famished and greedily consumed the contents of four thalis—the noon and evening meals for two persons—which the servant had left inside the hut. After rinsing his mouth with water and washing his hands, Gopal hurried back to the tamarind tree. He could hardly wait to resume his meditation. This time there was no pain above the anus but an immediate influx of light. The halo of brilliant bluish light, however, did not stay for long, dissolving into a myriad small dots, like milk curdling into particles. Gopal could see these points of light, some of them moving in playful spirals, shimmering throughout the heavens of his body whose outline was rapidly fading. This time when he returned to his body and opened his eyes the vision persisted even as it changed its form. He did not see the familiar landscape of the garden but rows and rows of minute particles of light stacked on top of each other, an unmoving wall made of glowing dots. He found himself walking toward this wall of light, puzzled whether he was following the path or the path was following him. He felt a light drizzle, no more than the wisp of a spray, on his face. He looked up to see delicate drops of liquid light falling gently from a luminous cloud covering the moon.

Meditation now filled most of his days and nights. In the morning he would hurry through his bath, bolt down a little rice and curds from the sumptuous meals the Dhamani women insisted on sending him, and sleep for a couple of hours during the last quarter of the night. The rest of the time he meditated. Except for the servant who came every day with the food and cleaned the hut and Dhamani who came thrice a week in the afternoon, content to sit quietly for a while in 'father's' presence, Gopal was alone. Nangta had sent a message through Dhamani that he would be away for a fortnight. 'If I do not go away, how will I ever return?' was the only explanation he wanted to be given to the disciple. Gopal wished the guru was there. He wanted to ask him, 'What is this light? Where does it come from? Why does it take various forms?' But he did not really miss him; the guru was all-pervasive even in his absence.

Gopal found that it took very little effort to meditate. On the contrary, meditation was now forcing itself upon him. He meditated almost involuntarily, needing only to close his eyes and repeat 'Guru Om' a few times before he found himself in the now familiar circle of light. The halo did not last long, though, changing into leaping, lustrous clouds or luminous currents that swirled and eddied. The ecstatic intoxication accompanying his first meditative efforts was now often absent, the newer visions more often than not characterized by violent movement rather than by blissful peace. Their luminosity also had a darker hue, more reddish than blue. In the most recent visions, it seemed as if a jet of molten copper dashed against the crown of his skull and fell in a shower of sparks all around him—a spectacular fireworks on a vast scale, that evoked awe but no joy.

Two days before Nangta's return, Gopal saw a red glow, like the aura on the horizon after sunset, emerge from his body during the morning meditation. The aura was roughly his own size and its emergence was accompanied by strong sexual sensations. For the first time, the 'Guru Om' mantra vanished. His mind was invaded by frankly sexual images: a naked couple, the man's thick penis going in and out of the woman who lay on her back, her eyes rolled up in ecstasy; a naked woman on her knees, her long black hair hanging down to her buttocks and, her arms wrapped around Nangta, sucking his aroused organ; a chorus of voices, male and female, saying two words over and over again in a rising crescendo—'Cunt!' 'Cock!' 'Cunt!' 'Cock!'

For someone as naturally pure as Gopal who had not looked carnally at a woman even in a dream, the sexual invasion was utterly horrifying. A wave of self-loathing swept over him as he struggled to dam the cascade of lascivious images, shut his ears to the lewd sounds. His penis was agonizingly erect, straining against the thin muslin loincloth. It was beyond the reach of his will, peremptory in its demand for a soft sheath, for being squeezed and stroked. Fortunately, all this turmoil had not disturbed his meditative posture. His legs remained firmly locked, his hands rigid.

'Guru Om,' he began again, closing his eyes. 'Guru Om.' For some time, he was again at peace as the devotional mood overcame the sexual state of the mind, enabling him to enter bhava samadhi again. This time the light that appeared had the glow of burning embers. It was the flare of passion fuelled by the flesh, whispering urgently through the senses. And then, within this crimson aura he saw one of the young prostitutes he had visited with Dhamani. The girl was naked, a fiery sheen on her flat, slightly hollow belly and firm breasts. She sat in front of him. He could almost touch her. Her legs were spread apart and her right hand was rubbing against the slit of her shaven pudendum. She was looking at him and laughing. He could not get rid of her. If he opened his eyes he saw her without; if he closed them, he saw her within. His penis was reacting violently. Its tip had ripped through the loin cloth and was pressing against his navel. Overwhelmed by shame and confusion, he rushed back to the safety of the hut. The woman ran after him, laughing all the while. He lay down on Nangta's spot on the floor, curled in the foetal position, incessantly chanting 'Guru Om', the mantra a lifeline to keep him from sinking into the sexual mire, its repetition an armour against the onrush of disgusting thoughts. His body was on fire, his throat scorched. Streams of cold sweat poured down his face but the heat kept getting intense. It seemed as if molten lava was rampaging through his body, blistering his organs and tissues. He walked out to the well, pulled up a bucket of water and poured it over his head but the heat did not let up. The only way to end the agony was to jump into the well.

Two days earlier than he intended, Nangta returned to

Jaipur as abruptly as he had departed. After initiating Gopal, he had decided to leave him alone for a while. The guru could only be a guide, not a crutch, and Nangta wanted Gopal to explore the various realms of meditation by himself. He had to fully experience their wonders, and terrors, and not seal off their impact by a premature search for explanations that the guru could provide. Nangta had not gone far. He had got off the bus at Amber and was staying in a small, dilapidated temple at the outskirts of the town. He was waiting till it was time for him to return.

When Nangta entered the garden and saw Gopal standing at the edge of the well, peering down, he knew what had happened.

'Ram Das!' he cried out Gopal's monastic name.

Gopal did not hear. Sweat ran down his shaved head. His body was the colour of a clay pot newly fired in the kiln. He was panting hard.

As soon as he felt Nangta's arms around his body, Gopal felt the heat and agitation seep out through his limbs. Nangta's own body was cool, smelling faintly of morning dew on jasmine buds. Gopal could not imagine how the guru could tolerate his rank smell without being thoroughly disgusted and tried to break out of the embrace. Nangta let him go but placed a firm arm around his shoulder and gently led him to the shaded spot under the tamarind tree.

Nangta did not need Gopal to tell him anything, he knew exactly what had transpired. He explained to Gopal that the sexual excitement which had caused him such agony was part of a change taking place in his whole system, a process that expelled lust, annihilating the sexual urge.

'Forever?' Gopal asked, still recovering from the shock.

'That is probable in your case, Ram Das. Remember, sex is not such a big problem when one is young. It is much harder for a monk when he is older, when the body panics and revolts, demanding its due as it senses the shutting of the gate. It is then that Kama within the blood comes streaming up from who knows what unknowable depths. I have seen many an old monk locked in a silent struggle against the sudden revival of lust that rouses the body to infinite uproar, sweeping away the frail dams built by the mind. I have seen some place a noose around the neck, tightening it painfully whenever they felt a quickening of carnal desire. Many succumb but a true ascetic starts all over again. He falls only to rise and only the ignorant draw a line between rise and fall.'

'And the naked woman?'

'Ah, our Mother, She is indeed a mischievous One,' Nangta smiled. 'So playful. Ensnaring even a heart as pure as yours in the web of Her illusion. You did not recognize the Great Goddess? The mother from whose womb the universe is born? The goddess Kundalini? She seemed naked to you because you yourself were naked, lacking true knowledge. What is the difference between a naked and a clad woman, anyway?'

He then touched the top of Gopal's head with his tongue, as if tasting the salty skin, and caressed his face.

'Remember, She assumes all forms, beautiful or ugly, young or old, virgin or whore—all is Her in Her fullness.'

As Gopal told his disciples many years afterwards, since that day he had never felt sexual excitement. 'The turmoil it caused is only a memory,' he said. 'Sexual visions are now like any other—all lead to God. One day, I saw Shiva and Shakti fucking. Enchanted and entranced, I saw the god and goddess—matter and energy, stasis and change—everywhere around me. I saw them in human beings, animals, plants, each one either male or female and all of them busy fucking. Another time I was going to Dhamani's house when, in the middle of Johri bazaar, I entered samadhi at the sight of a dog and bitch copulating. What I saw in the vagina of the bitch was the face of the Goddess. And,' he added with an impish smile, 'sometimes when meditating, instead of the solemn mantra I go on repeating the word "cunt". The vision I am granted at such times is of the Brahmayoni, the cosmic vagina, glowing in a tawny fleshy light which comes from somewhere deep within and I blissfully sink into it.'

Once the crisis had passed, Gopal's progress through the various realms of consciousness was rapid, reinforcing Nangta's faith in his prodigious spiritual talent. He could now enter bhava samadhi almost at will, needing but a few seconds of meditation before the celestial portals opened. The visions, full of fresh wonders, took him deeper and deeper into the hidden heart of God. He followed Nangta's simple prescriptions for the protection of the body, the indispensable container for the flights of the soul.

'Never meditate long on an empty stomach. Take a light meal every three hours. To counteract the bodily heat generated by meditation and prolonged trances, follow the good advice Madhavacharya gave you: rub sandalwood paste on the soles of your feet and wear a garland of fresh, fragrant flowers every time you sit down for meditation.'

With each passing day, the radiance of the visions was also subtly refining his senses. Whenever he happened to look up, the azure dome of the sky had a purity of colour he had never seen before. The change was taking place in every object that entered his field of vision. Each seemed garbed in a new-found beauty, wrapped in a silvery sheen, its colours resplendent. Late in the evening, when he walked through the bazaars, the lamps in the shops and in the houses glowed with a new brilliance and the objects they illuminated had a lustre only partly borrowed from the lamps. Sounds became more defined, possessing amplification and tonal qualities which at first he found disconcerting. The birdsong of the koel and the starling to which he awoke in the morning had a melody and music he had never heard before, while the blaring horns of the trucks that passed on the road outside so grated on his ears that he had to press his palms against them to keep out their disagreeable harshness. When he sang, which he sometimes did when Dhamani came for a visit and begged him to, the additional sweetness to his voice made even Nangta, who otherwise disapproved of music's spontaneity and its fine-tuned language of feelings, misty-eyed, while the jeweller wept openly, fat tears running in and out of the craters of his pock-marked face.

Gopal's inner vision was changing even more radically than outer perception. His dreams became extraordinarily vivid. And though their stories continued to retain their dream character, lacking any apparent coherence or continuity, the images took on some of the characteristics of his visions: vistas of a vastness and magnificence seldom seen in real life and a luminous background against which the nocturnal dramas played themselves out. When he closed his eyes, especially before going to sleep, he could clearly see a silvery light, delicately tinged with gold, inside the cranial cavity and spreading across his forehead. Sometimes, if he concentrated enough, he could perceive the inner topography of his body, see lucent currents of energy flowing through the network of nerves in the body. His thought images became bright and vivid and every object recalled to memory possessed the same distinctiveness, in shape and colour, as in its concrete form in the real world. The senses of taste, smell and touch, too, were becoming more sensitive and acute, though here the changes were less marked than in the case of sight. Nangta only smiled indulgently when Gopal reported on these changes.

'Ah, you have begun to experience your experiences more fully. But don't take the visions too seriously. Remember that the goal remains a total, complete experiencing of experience, full knowledge stripped of the illusion in which most people sleepwalk through life: the knowledge of nirvikalpa samadhi, where one finds out that there is neither the knower nor the known. Of course, if ever that time should come, there will be no One left to make this discovery.'

And Nangta laughed, enjoying the look of bafflement on his beloved disciple's face.

Chapter Twelve

Nangta was a fearsome apparition as he rushed towards the gate, hair flying and iron tongs raised, shouting incoherent threats that sounded quite murderous. The group of villagers, three men and two women, scattered in panic before turning and running back, milling in front of the gate in a mêlée of bright colours—the orange and crimson of the turbans clashing with the yellow and green of the women's odhnis, as each tried to squeeze out of the narrow opening at the same time.

He was chuckling as he walked back, having broken off the attack midway to the gate. An austere yet essentially gentle man, Nangta only acted the part of the irascible sadhu, unpredictable and quick to take offence. He did this because rumours of a great guru and his disciple practicing secret meditations, locked in a fierce struggle with demons and deities from whom they were trying to wrest supernatural powers, had begun to attract the curious. Dhamani had promised to deploy a watchman to keep the intruders out but had yet to find someone willing to take the job.

Nangta spent his evenings next to the well where he kept a fire burning throughout the day. Besides serving sacred purposes, the fire also provided him with burning pieces of coal to light his clay pipe which, given the raw, untreated tobacco he smoked, repeatedly kept going out. In later years, whenever Gopal was asked about his mild addiction to tobacco, he attributed his fondness for smoking to those evenings in Dhamani's garden when Nangta and he had companionably shared the pipe while the guru talked and the disciple listened, his occasional question never intending to dispute but only to clarify.

'Why do you meditate for hours early in the morning and again at night when you have already reached the highest state of samadhi, have become perfect?' Gopal asked once.

Nangta pointed to his brass eating bowl (the one made from a human skull was merely a pedagogic device) which he polished each day and kept shining. This was one of his few possessions, the others being his clay pipe, a pair of tongs, and a coarse sheet of cloth with which he covered himself on winter nights.

'See how bright it looks,' he said. 'But what would happen if I did not polish it? It would lose its lustre. The mind is like the bowl. It also accumulates dirt if not polished daily by the practice of meditation.'

Their conversations were not always serious but they were never personal. Nangta did not talk about who he was and what he did before he became a sadhu, more than thirty years ago. He regarded his earlier life as belonging to someone with no connection to who he was now, professing a radical discontinuity in the sense of 'I' which Gopal found fascinating. He showed little interest in Gopal's childhood in Deogarh. He was more curious about his Galta years. These, he believed, had fostered an excessive emotionalism that was inimical to the direct experience of the Self, of a formless God. He poked gentle fun at Gopal's continuing devotion to Rama and Sita. In the mornings, when after his bath Gopal chanted 'Hari Rama! Hari Rama!!', accompanying the chanting with a vigorous clapping of his hands—a childhood habit he carried over from the morning pujas with his mother—Nangta would call out, 'Ah, making chapatis again!' But would then add kindly, 'It doesn't matter. The sound of chanting helps to still the mind.' He barely tolerated Dhamani's visits since the jeweller encouraged Gopal to sing the glories of the Lord. In Nangta's view, the singing further anchored Gopal's mind in devotional fervour whereas the next step required that he transcend all devotion to personal deities and even to Nangta; that he now kill the guru.

These days Gopal's meditations were without any sign of turmoil; he entered the meditative trance at will. But as his meditation deepened, his visions of light and space, accompanied by intense joy and an inexpressible sense of freedom, often led to visions of the Goddess. Most of the time the Divine Mother appeared in the form of Sita which he had encountered in the garden of Galta. Nangta had to wrench him away from the contemplation of her beauty and the utter bliss her presence evoked by bringing him back to body consciousness. She stood in the way of the samadhi Nangta wanted for him.

Each day Nangta exhorted Gopal to free his mind of all its functions. When he sat down to meditate, Gopal could easily empty his mind and withdraw it from all objects, shut off the flow of thought. But as soon as he did so, the light appeared and with it the entrancing visions.

'No, it cannot be done,' he said to Nangta one evening. 'I cannot free my mind from the visions it craves, from the forms in which it takes such delight. I cannot make it dive into the Self behind it.'

They were sitting on the floor of the hut, facing each other. It was just after sunset but not yet dark. In the trees, resident parrots and starlings were noisily settling down for the night. A light breeze, scented with the smoke from cooking fires burning cow-dung cakes, came in through the open door.

'What do you mean it can't be done?' Nangta scolded. 'What nonsense!'

He then looked around the hut and seeing the pair of tongs on the floor beside him, picked them up and lunged forward, stabbing Gopal in the forehead with the sharp end of one of the prongs.

'There!' he said. 'Collect the mind here. At this point.'

In spite of the sharp pain between the eyebrows and the drops of blood that trickled down his nose, Gopal obediently closed his eyes and began to meditate. The pain vanished as he turned his mind away from it. The unearthly light began to fill his vision and then the Goddess herself appeared, her face graciously inclined, a faint smile on her lips.

'This time,' he said when he recounted the experience to his disciples, 'I mentally picked up the sword of knowledge and pierced the holy form of the Divine Mother. Every function of my mind stopped. It became utterly motionless.'

Nangta sat beside him for a long time as night fell and the garden became still. He then stepped outside the hut, pulling the door shut behind him. He put pieces of coal into the fire and sat next to the well, smoking, waiting for Gopal's call. Morning came and still there was no sign of life from the hut. Nangta drew water from the well, bathed, meditated, ate, smoked, slept. Day passed into night. At the end of three days, he entered the hut. Gopal was sitting in the same posture in which he had left him, rigid, unmoving, like the stone statue of a meditating Buddha. Nangta felt the carotid artery in Gopal's neck and then placed his palm over his heart. The signs of the vital force were so slight as to be nonexistent; Gopal was as good as dead to the external world. Nangta checked for other signs of nirvikalpa samadhi and was satisfied. Gopal's mind, calm, motionless, was indeed merged in the underlying Self that existed, though hidden, through all the varied states of the mind. His mind had become a part of Brahman. Sonorous sounds of 'Hari Om!' filled the hut as Nangta calmly went about the task of awakening the disciple to the world, bring him down from a state of pure consciousness to the contaminated one that interacted with the world. He rubbed ghee into Gopal's back, massaging it from the neck down to the end of the spine above the coccyx and then into his legs, from the knees downwards to the soles of his feet. Slowly, he felt Gopal's body come alive under his hands as his consciousness was coaxed back from the plane of samadhi to the realm of 'I' and 'mine'.

Nangta's task was now over and he could resume his wanderings. He had stayed too long anyway. And suddenly he felt a strong agitation grip his heart at the thought of leaving the boy. After what had happened between them, he was not surprised at the feeling but at its strength. He had not expected it to wrench his composure. Thirty years of sustained spiritual discipline had not cleansed his heart of its grasping nature, purified his love of the urge to be close to its object. There he was, identifying the two of them with their respective bodies and thus seeing Gopal and himself as separate entities which could come near or be parted. Where was his hard-won knowledge that everyone and everything in the universe is grounded in the same underlying Self? What had happened to the realization 'I am Thou'? Where was the perfection Gopal had so trustingly attributed to him? It was transitory, to be striven for even when one thought one had attained it. He would leave Jaipur the very next day.

In the morning, Nangta was awakened by a sharp pain in his gut. Gopal was still submerged in the deep sleep that follows samadhi. His face had the innocence of a newborn child who knows everything there is to know. Nangta went out, bathed, and then sat in meditation, turning his mind away from the pain. Whenever he was conscious, though, the pain was still there. It turned out to be a severe attack of dysentery and Nangta had to postpone his departure.

'Tomorrow,' he thought. 'I'll certainly leave tomorrow.'

The sickness persisted. All he could eat was two tablespoons of boiled rice. After five days of agony he finally agreed to take the medicine Dhamani had brought him. The medicine did not help. His strong body became weak, wilting visibly. His calm and tranquil mind, accustomed to samadhi, was made more and more aware of the body by the wrenching pain gnawing at his intestines. Nangta fought against it by heaping scorn on his body, calling it that 'rotten cage of flesh, gristle and bone, full of blood and bile, a filth-producing factory.' It should not matter to him if the body suffered, became emaciated, was even destroyed. Had he not seen and felt clearly, without a shadow of doubt, that *he* was *not* the body? He could still turn his mind away from that wretched appendage which caused so much trouble. One night, as Gopal was massaging his feet, trying to ease his suffering and help him sleep, the pain became so excruciating that he could not lie quietly. He had to keep sitting up, bent double in agony. He tried to still his mind through meditation, but just when he had brought it to rest it would turn sharply towards the pain. He tried again and again but without success. For the first time, meditation failed him and Nangta was in despair. Tears ran down his face, not of pain but of humiliation. Gopal took his guru in his arms.

'I shall ask Mother to relieve you of this suffering,' he said lovingly and closed his eyes to meditate. Of course, when Sita appeared he was so absorbed in the contemplation of her presence that there was no one left to ask. It did not matter, though. When he returned to consciousness, he found Nangta sleeping peacefully, his head in Gopal's lap. By the morning, the disease had disappeared as mysteriously as it had come.

'Sometimes I feel that Nangta deliberately fell sick to teach me an important lesson,' Gopal was to confide in his disciples. 'Knowledge of the Self is not something you get to keep once you have achieved it. You may shut your eyes and try to persuade yourself that there is no thorn and no prick but as soon as your finger touches the thorn, it hurts and you cry out in pain. You may try to persuade your mind that there is no birth or death, no vice or virtue, no pain or pleasure, no hunger or thirst—that you are the immutable Self. But as soon as your body falls prey to some disease, you forget all about the immutable Self. Self-knowledge is constantly in jeopardy, to be won over and over again.'

Dhamani had decided to build a temple in the garden. He personally supervised the construction and came to the garden every day to watch his marble offering to 'father' take shape. Gopal had expressed only one wish: the hut in which he had lived with Nangta be kept unaltered. Dhamani did not insist that 'father' stay at his house during the six months it would take for the temple to be built. Gopal was to temporarily live in the Govindraja temple near by where he could be properly looked after. He was concerned at 'father's' withdrawn state after Nangta's departure. He did not sing anymore and his open face was now closed, his eyes empty of their normal lustre.

During the next six months Gopal lived in a small cell on the premises of the Govindraja temple. His cell was one of seven in a row at the back of the hundred-pillared hall, a raised stone platform in front of the shrine, open on three sides, its roof supported by a forest of slender, carved pillars. He never entered the inner shrine. He did not need to. The cell was bare, its floor made of large slabs of stone. The only opening was a rotting wooden door, sagging on its hinges, which could never be fully opened or shut. Here, for six months Gopal was in a continuous state of samadhi which a normal human being cannot bear for more than twenty-one days, the body then falling away like a dry leaf from a tree. All this time his body was utterly neglected, unwashed, his hair growing long and matted with dust. He did not bother to tie a loin cloth. He seemed unaware that he had a body at all. The thoughts around its maintenance—the necessity of sleeping, eating, defecating—never crossed his mind. It was not that Gopal was unconscious for six months but only that his consciousness of the external world was intermittent and tenuous. He sometimes opened his eyes and found that it was dark and sometimes that it was light. That was all he knew of the passing of day and night as time came to a stop. Dhamani came every afternoon, bringing him food. By striking his back and shoulders repeatedly and shouting his name, he would sometimes succeed in making Gopal open his eyes. The moment he saw signs of a waking consciousness appear, he would thrust some food into Gopal's mouth. Thus on some days a little nourishment found its way to Gopal's stomach and on others it did not. The servant boy had to help him if he ever wanted to go to the latrine, for Gopal had barely the strength to stand up unaided. He would raise himself up a few inches and then sink back again, weak and dizzy. He had to try several times before he could finally stand on his feet.

When the rains came, the cell became damp and crawled with large black ants. They preyed upon him until his thighs and legs were covered with sores oozing blood and pus. He remained unmoved by the torment they caused, and also indifferent to mosquito bites. Dhamani beseeched him to leave the cell and shift to his house but Gopal gave no sign of having heard. The jeweller brought him clean sheets to sit or lie on and thus at least partially protect himself against the insects but the sheets lay unused in a corner, smelling of mildew. The marks left on his legs by the sores remained till the end of his life.

Later, after the temple was built and the first disciples had begun to gather around him, they occasionally saw him enter nirvikalpa samadhi but never for more than twenty-four hours at a stretch. As he grew older, he seemed to return to his devotional beginnings, preferring the ecstatic trances of bhava samadhi where a trace of 'I' remained to enjoy the bliss of Divine presence and the radiant yet grave visions it sent.

'I would rather eat sugar than become sugar,' he would say with a laugh. But the nirvikalpa experiences, especially the one after Nangta's departure, had permanently altered the state of his consciousness. One morning, a disciple was massaging his legs. After about half an hour of the massage, Baba, as he was now called, suddenly said, 'I vaguely feel something is being massaged.' At the time, he was neither in a trance nor in samadhi.

Dhamani died in the summer of 1961, ten years after the completion of the temple and at the end of a hopeful decade in Independent India's history. The Congress Party, under Gandhi's chosen heir, Jawaharlal Nehru, reigned supreme in all parts of the country. It had only recently begun to acquire a reputation for corruption which would become its hallmark in the coming decades. Cynics were still in a miniscule minority and the country was enthralled by its handsome and charismatic Prime Minister, an admirer of the Soviet Union, whose vision for India was a 'democratic collectivism' and 'a socialistic pattern of society'. The second Five-Year Plan had just ended and work on huge steelworks and large dams, which Nehru called the 'temples of modern India', had begun.

Jaipur, too, was changing. The magnificent city walls had been demolished to widen the roads. The arcades under which pedestrians could walk in the shade in the bazaars were now encroached upon by shopkeepers, forcing people out onto the road where they had to dodge the motley traffic of trucks, tongas, camel-drawn carts, cars, buses, bicycles and the cycle-rickshaws. Slums were sprouting inside the old city as were unplanned colonies outside.

All these years, Dhamani had conscientiously taken care of the temple's upkeep and Baba's sparse personal needs. In the last months of his illness, a rare blood disease, he handed over his jewellery business to his younger brother and spent most of his days in the company of 'father'. Near the end, when he could no longer walk, or even barely stand, he was brought to the garden in his new Fiat car that had replaced the horse carriage and would be carried in by two servants. For a couple of hours he would lie on a mattress in a corner of the pavilion, half-listening to Baba's discourse. His eyes, though, fading away like those of an old dog slowly dying, left 'father's' face only for the brief periods the lids drooped in sleep.

One afternoon, Dhamani did not come at all and Ram

Das knew the end was near. That evening, he dismissed the disciples early and walked to the jeweller's house. Dhamani lay in bed, his wife squatting silently on the floor, fanning him with a hand-held bamboo fan. The portly jeweller was thin now, almost skeletal. Its thick underlying layer of fat burnt off by the disease, his skin sagged around his large frame. It hung in pock-marked folds under his chin. His palm was hot and dry as Ram Das tenderly took it into both his hands. Dhamani's drained yet feverishly bright eyes looked imploringly into his. Ram Das sensed the doubts bubbling up in Dhamani's soul which would not let him drift off into the final sleep. He brought his mouth close to the jeweller's ear, hoping he could still hear.

'Do not doubt its existence, my friend. There is an immortal Self in the depths of our being—beyond the body or the mind. There have been Yogis whose body did not decay with death, sometimes for as long as eighteen days, in spite of the cessation of all brain activity. What else kept their bodies fresh but the working of the ineffable Self? Go peacefully, without a shadow of doubt.'

He didn't know if the jeweller heard him. Dhamani's eyes were closed by the time Baba ended his short speech. He sat by the bedside through the night till Dhamani passed away in the early hours of the morning, just when the first bells began to peal in the temples all over the city. Except for a last rattling struggle for breath, his death was peaceful.

Baba

A man goes far to find out what he is—
Death of the self in a long tearless night,
All natural shapes blazing unnatural life.

—THEODOR ROETHKE,
In a Dark Time

Chapter Thirteen

Trilok Nath had been playing tennis at the Jaipur Club around the same time his son was cycling home with his friends from the Sitaram temple after that first encounter with Baba Ram Das. He had just thrown up the ball to serve, squinting his eyes against the setting sun, when he collapsed on the court from a massive brain haemorrhage. He was driven straight to the Sawai Mansingh Hospital where, befitting his status as an IAS officer and secretary to the Government of Rajasthan, he received immediate attention from the hospital's senior-most doctors. Trilok Nath did not regain consciousness and died two hours later. The hospital administration reduced the death formalities to a minimum and the body was brought back home by nine in the evening. The living room was emptied of all furniture, the carpets rolled up and the body kept on blocks of ice on the floor in preparation for the cremation next morning.

The arrival of the family priest a little after sunrise, followed by that of the barber a few minutes later, was the signal for the women to leave the room. Vivek was surprised at how calm he could remain even as he watched his mother, her eyes red and swollen, shuffle out of the room, her piteous sobbing of the night having subsided into silent exhaustion.

'The trick to get through the cremation and the rest of the day without breaking down and collapsing into a puddle is to keep your attention resolutely away from the rush of images from the past and also to stop it from wandering into thoughts of the future. Your attention needs to be focussed on what is happening within the confines of this particular space, the living room of the house, now stripped of all familiarity by death. Do not try to pick up the sound of your mother's wails from the loud crying which has resumed outside. Watch the two men in the corner who are preparing the bamboo bier and covering it with straw. Look at the barber shaving off your father's hair. After he finishes, the priest will assist you in washing the body. Remember, it is a corpse, dead flesh, not the father you revered and adored. All you have to do is to take it one step at a time: right foot, left foot; left foot, right foot. Separate the observer from the actor. Now, take the moist piece of cloth the priest is handing to you to sponge the body in a ritual bath.'

Vivek could not help but recoil from the first contact with the ice-cold flesh. For a few seconds his eyes, with a will of their own, refused to be averted from his father's cock, the mighty paternal phallus of his boyhood imagination now shrivelled and flopping against a faintly blue thigh as the men pulled down the shorts.

After the sponging was complete, the body wrapped in a coarse white cloth, with the face left uncovered, Vivek helped to tie the body down securely to the bier with thick jute strings so it wouldn't shift or slide off when the bier was lifted onto the shoulders of the four men who would carry the corpse to the municipal hearse parked outside. The concentration required by the task was just what Vivek needed to keep the flow of time dammed. The mourners—neighbours, his father's colleagues and their wives, looking strangely unfamiliar without the expression of self-importance they normally wore in public—began to fill the room. Vivek watched them help themselves to garlands of marigold and rose petals that were heaped on silver trays in one corner of the room and place them on the bier. Then they touched his father's covered feet in silent leave-taking. Vivek carefully avoided looking at his mother who had sat down on the floor at the foot of the bier. She was surrounded by a group of women clad in cotton saris in various shades of white who had slipped easily into ritual grieving. It was a noisy, mechanical ritual: slapping their foreheads repeatedly, the women wailed in a shrill chorus—'Why have you left us?', 'Oh, where have you gone?'. Their cries drowned out the priest's murmured chanting and the scratchy music from a record of devotional songs playing on the family's old gramaphone. 'Right foot, left foot,' Vivek kept repeating to himself. 'Left foot, right foot.

The sun was high by the time the municipal hearse, followed by the Ambassdors and Fiats crammed full with mourners—all men—reached the cremation ground at the foot of Moti Doongri, the palace-fort built at the beginning of the century by the rulers of Jaipur for pleasure rather than protection, for love, not war. Perched on a rocky outcrop of the Aravallis, scattered orange and purple bougainvillea peeping through its delicate crenellations, Moti Doongri loomed above the cremation ground. Perhaps the pleasure of romantic trysts in its inner apartments was heightened by the daily demonstration of the body's impermanence below.

'*All you have to do is to hold yourself together for the next hour. Right foot: the body will be untied and placed on the pyre. Left foot: you will pull off the cloth covering the upper part of the body and scatter basil leaves and pieces of sweet-smelling sandalwood over it. Then the hardest part: going around the pyre once with a flaming bundle of dry grass, then lighting the fire near the head, hastening your father's consummation with the flames by pouring ladles of ghee on the burning pyre. Do not dwell on the last image. The breaking open of the skull with a long pole when the body is half burnt to let the soul escape. Your father's soul. The soul of a man who did not believe in the existence of one. An atheist who loved life and was always impatient with the rites that mark its going. Do not think too much about this. These are just rites, needed so that your father will not become a ghost to haunt those he loved most. Ghosts only haunt houses where something has been left undone. Right foot, left foot. Be patient with the rites. They are only meant to hammer the utter irrevocability of his death into your obdurate soul, compelling you to let go.*'

And then the tears came, in a rush, flooding his soul, streaming down his face, filling the abyss that was his heart.

A couple of weeks later, when most of the death ceremonies meant to ease the passage of his father's soul into the world of ancestral spirits were complete and the household was limply setting up new routines that excluded the familiar requirements of the departed member, Vivek discovered what he had always known, that he was now expected to provide for the family's financial needs. The turban that the family priest had tied around his head at the conclusion of the fourth-day ceremony was not only symbolic of the son succeeding his father but entailed the discharge of some immediate responsibilities. Vivek was expected to sort out his father's financial affairs and expeditously arrange for the money needed each month to meet the household expenses.

As he set about unscrambling Trilok Nath's chaotic finances, Vivek noted a subtle change take place in the behaviour of his mother and grand-aunt. Their earlier indulgence toward him was now tinged with deference; he was no longer just a son or a nephew but also the freshly anointed head of the family, with the ultimate responsibility for its survival and welfare. His grand-uncle Kali Prasad was not expected to be of much help. Kali Prasad's interest in the outside world had always been in terms of how well or badly it satisfied his desires. Over the years, even this view of the world being a mere caterer to his pleasures had narrowed further. The outer world had now shrunk to those of its elements which either stimulated the palate or were pleasing to the skin. All he looked forward to during the day, which he spent sitting in a comfortable cane chair under a mango tree in the garden during the winter or reclining against soft bolsters in his darkened room in summer, listening to the old gramophone records of his youth, were his meals and the daily oil massage.

Kali Prasad became truly animated only at meal times. His rheumy eyes glittered and his otherwise fidgety attention was fiercely focussed on the food. The expression of bliss on his face while he ate darkened if he detected the slightest flaw in the cooking or serving of food. The least uncertainty in the blending of the spices, the malformed texture of a vegetable that was a little overcooked, a roti which was not fluffed out to its fullest potential, provoked sarcastic comment.

The source of his other pleasure was his skin, still soft and smooth in spite of his seventy years. Punctually at eleven in the morning, the maid entered his room for the daily mustard-oil massage while Kali Prasad reclined naked in bed, reading the morning newspaper. The massage lasted a long time, sometimes for well over an hour. From the way it was talked about, or rather, ignored by the family, the massage constituted another one of those adult secrets from which the young were excluded. Vivek once overheard the maid complain to the cook after she had finished the day's session and was drinking a cup of tea in the kitchen.

'Nothing happened, although my hand is tired from all that massaging. The master's thing kept lying on his thigh like a dead mouse.'

Vivek had tried to bring the gravity of their situation home to his grand-uncle.

'I think there is the provident fund and the money due from his life insurance policy. That is about all. Papa did not save. A few hundred rupees in the bank account. No fixed deposits with the bank, no shares.'

'He was like me,' Kali Prasad said, smiling fondly at the memory of his nephew who was also like a son. 'Never paid much regard to money. Spent it all. Enjoyed himself.'

'What are we going to do?' Vivek persisted. 'We can put the insurance and provident fund money into a bank fixed deposit but the monthly interest it will earn is far short of our expenses.'

But the old man had already switched off.

'Oh, you will think of something,' he said vaguely. 'You are a clever boy. Now, where is that woman? It is time for my massage.'

As Vivek expected, the women were more sympathetic, although they too left him alone with the task of finding a durable solution to the problem.

'We shall do whatever you think is right,' his mother said with a touching confidence in her son's abilities. 'We can always move to a smaller place and let the cook and the maid go.'

'Yes,' Sharada Devi concurred. 'Your mother is young and it is not as if she has any other work to do . . . besides her puja, of course.'

'Maji,' Maheshwari began hotly, joining the engagement, 'as far as my puja is concerned . . .'

Vivek's friends recognized the critical nature of his situation and tried to help.

'My sister has just entered Maharani's College. Since she went to school in our *thikana* near Shekhawati, all her education has been in Hindi. Now with her subjects at the college level being taught in English, she needs a tutor who can help her with English,' Kamal offered.

'But what about his own studies?' Nemi Chand objected. 'The BA exams are coming up and he has already missed a month of classes.'

'No, no,' Vivek said. 'We need the money more than any extra marks I may or may not get in the exam. What can I do with a philosophy degree anyway? Even to be a school teacher you need to go through a special teacher's training course.'

The other three boys looked uncomfortable. They knew that Trilok Nath had planned that his son join the prestigous St Stephen's College in Delhi after graduation, take his Master's degree in philosophy and then appear for the civil service examinations. He had hoped that Vivek would follow him into the Indian Administrative Service and go on to make a career even more brilliant than his own.

'This fellow is lucky,' Suresh said, poking a finger in Kamal's rib, trying to lighten the gloom that seemed to have descended on their small group. 'All these young Rajputs who have not turned their family homes into hotels go off to work as supervisors in the tea estates of Assam.'

'Well, what more can you ask from a job?' Kamal agreed good-naturedly. 'To work on a tea estate gives a Rajput all he needs: outdoor life, riding, some hunting, and plenty of liquor in the evening.'

'And the company of dusky, young female tea-pickers at night,' Nemi Chand added.

Vivek smiled but did not join in the hoots of laughter that greeted the sally. The others really did not expect him to. Ever since they had known him, he had been a serious young man who barely tolerated their sexual banter and showed no interest in the romantic escapades that dominated their hormone-fuelled imaginations.

During the next couple of weeks, Vivek discovered that the family's financial situation was more than worrying; it was disastrous. Going carefully through his father's papers, he found that Trilok Nath had taken out a large loan against his life insurance policy and had also borrowed heavily from his Provident Fund. Vivek's plan of investing in a bank fixed deposit that would yield a regular though modest interest was no longer feasible. The financial crunch was not going to come sometime in the future but was already upon them. Although Kali Prasad made voluble protests and sulked by not appearing at the dining table and asking for his food to be sent to his room, the services of the cook, the maid and the gardener were immediately terminated. Vivek stopped going to the wrestling gymnasium. After the intial glow of sacrifice had dimmed, he discovered that he missed his morning wrestling routine, that it had also become a physical need. But there was no other way. They simply could not afford to spend so much money on the milk, ghee and almonds required in a wrestler's daily diet. The family could stay on in the house, which belonged to the state, for another three months but Vivek did not know what they would do afterwards. Most landlords required six months of rent in advance. Even for a very modest accommodation, this added up to a considerable sum of money which they simply did not have.

Kamal's suggestion that Vivek tutor his sister had run into the objections of his parents that having a male tutor for their daughter would damage the girl's chances of marriage in their conservative Rajput community. Kamal tried his best, arguing that his friend was a serious young man who was a monk as far as interest in the opposite sex was concerned, but the parents remained unconvinced.

His father's colleagues, the 'uncles' who had enjoyed Trilok Nath's food and drink in the lavish parties he had thrown over the years, were sympathetic when he sought their help in finding work but the sympathy was not translated into active assistance.

'Leave your application and I'll see what can be done,' was the usual response, or some variation of it. When he persisted, turning up at their offices after every few days to find out if there had been any progress, he was more often than not turned away by an officious clerk with the response that the sahib was busy and could not see him.

The little money that now came in was when his mother sold one of her gold ornaments. At such times, Vivek became acutely aware of his helplessness, his failure as a man and a provider for the family. The hot shame that coursed through his body, making him want to hide from people, smothered any feeling of relief he may have felt at the fact that at least they would have enough to eat for the next few months. His mother tried to console him.

'Surrender to God's will, child,' she said. 'When an unfavorable period comes in one's life, all effort is futile. When God decrees that the time is ripe, then without even asking you will be showered with all that you ever wanted. Suffering purifies. It brings man nearer to God. That is why Kunti prayed to Krishna, "Bless us with endless adversity so that we shall never forget You."'

Her simple faith, about which he had sometimes affectionately teased her, now irritated him.

'Be quiet, mother!' he burst out one day. 'Such flights of fancy are sweet only to those who live in the lap of luxury. Talk of God and His ways is a mockery of the lives of people whose loved ones are close to starvation.'

He much preferred Sharada Devi's outbursts in which the old lady cursed an indifferent God and a heartless world ruled by selfishness that had no place in it for those who were down on their luck. Soon, he stopped going to college and began to avoid his friends. He could not bear the pity he imagined he saw in their eyes. He felt ashamed, resentful and close to tears whenever one of them offered to lend him money to tide over the bad times.

There were days when Vivek sneaked into the kitchen early in the morning to check on the supplies and found that there was not enough food available for everyone. He would then leave the house early, telling his mother that he was invited for lunch by one of his friends, so that the others could divide his share of the food between them. He would spend the morning cycling aimlessly through the bazaars and often end up in Ramnivas Gardens where he would lie on the grass under the shade of a tree, the distant thwack of the cricket bat striking the ball and the occasional cry of a white peacock from the nearby zoo the only intruders on his reveries. His mind was at peace at such times, though it was a peace based on the absence of despair rather than a presence of hope. Buddha was right, he felt. An involvement with the world only led to suffering; the small pleasures granted by a life of attachment to people and things were always purchased in a vastly undervalued currency of pain. Gradually, he was beginning to realize that one did not have to believe in God to find the life of a monk attractive. He remembered his mother's stories about his grandfather, the phrase he had muttered—'Who are you to me, woman?'—to the wife he was meeting again after twelve years. Perhaps, like his grandfather, he too was not born to earn money, to spend his life enmeshed in the web of family and children, enjoying life's transient pleasures but also enduring its infinitely greater sorrows. He began to seriously entertain the idea of becoming a sadhu. Not to embark on a search for God but to renounce any claims he and the world may have had on each other.

Increasingly, the image of Baba Ram Das began to insinuate itself into his thoughts, making him uncomfortably aware of his promise to visit the crazy sadhu again. No one seemed to know much about the man's past. There were rumours that he had once been a novice monk at Galta who had to leave because of some scandalous goings-on in the monastery many, many years ago. But the rumours did not seem to have affected the growing reverence in which he was held in the bazaars.

Chapter Fourteen

At eleven in the morning, Vivek found the Sitaram temple deserted. The dog that normally dozed at the gate had dragged itself to a cooler spot next to the well in the far left corner of the garden where it was curled under the meagre shade of a tamarind tree. Except for the low hum of bumblebees coming from the direction of the mango grove and the occasional horn of a passing truck on the road outside, the garden was shrouded in a drowsy silence. Vivek walked up to Baba's hut next to the well and nudging open the door, peered inside.

Baba was standing next to the small stone-latticed opening in the wall opposite the string bed. He saw Vivek come in but there was no immediate reaction; the beaming smile with which he had welcomed Vivek on his first visit was absent. He seemed to be in a strange mood, withdrawn, mumbling to himself, his eyes open yet veiled. 'This is not the right time for a visit,' Vivek thought, 'perhaps I should leave.' Suddenly, Baba stepped forward and motioning Vivek to sit on a low stool next to the bed, took two steps in his direction. 'Ah-ha!' Vivek thought, 'Here we go again. Another scene of lunacy will be enacted.' Baba sat down on the bed in front of Vivek, raised his right foot and placed it on the boy's lap. Instantly, before he even had time to be surprised, Vivek had the most frightening experience of his life. With his eyes open, he saw the bed, the walls, the stone-tiled floor, the curtained doorway and the ceiling of the hut snap adrift from their relation to each other and flutter loosely in space. An immense emptiness settled around him. He felt something deep within his body give a tug and cut loose. He was overwhelmed by an eerie feeling of being no longer what he used to be, his memories obliterated, the body a random collection of organs and limbs he did not recognize as his own. Loss of consciousness seemed imminent. He cried out, 'What are you doing? I am dying. I have my family, friends . . .'

He heard Baba laugh and felt the touch of his palm against his chest.

'Let it stop now,' he heard the sadhu say, as if to an unseen presence. 'It need not be done all at once. It will happen in due time.'

The terrible vision disappeared as suddenly as it had arisen. The room and its meagre furnishings were once again solid and moored to the earth, exactly as they were before. Baba's eyes had an odd glitter to them and he was still mumbling to himself. Unsteadily, not quite trusting his legs and his sense of balance, Vivek stood up to leave. Baba took his hands in his own, holding them tightly while he slowly emerged from his trance, shaking his head like a wet dog to clear the remnants of the trance. His face was glowing.

'You must come again soon,' he said with great affection.

'You cannot imagine how much I have missed you!'

Vivek's last image of Baba was that of his smile as he released his hands. It was the quick and open smile of a child looking up at the mother, animated with total love and brimming with unquestioning trust.

His mind was in turmoil as he cycled back to the city. He could not understand what had happened. Was that awful emptiness and the utter disconnectedness of things a revelation of the secret of the universe? Or of deep structures of his own psyche? Was it some kind of suggestion implanted in his mind by the Baba? He had read about mesmerism and hypnotism but believed that only a weak individual—not someone like him who possessed a strong will and firm convictions—could be hypnotized and thus bent to another's will. Whether revelation or hypnotic suggestion, could it be that this person who sometimes appeared quite mad and at others like a guileless child, had the power to shatter the cast of his mind and fashion it, like a ball of clay, into any shape he pleased? He must visit Baba again. He had to know the answer.

Vivek did not tell anyone about his experience, not even Kamal, whom he asked to accompany him to the Sitaram temple the very next afternoon. Kamal, who felt bad about failing to get his friend the tutor's position, readily agreed, relieved that Vivek finally seemed to be coming out of the shell into which he had withdrawn over the past few months. Vivek was mysterious about the purpose of their excursion.

'It is an experiment and I need you as a witness,' was all he would offer by way of explanation.

The only difference Kamal found from their first visit a couple of months ago was that Baba seemed to have gathered around him a few more young disciples, none more than fifteen or sixteen years old. The youths sat around him, looking fondly proprietorial, as he talked to the devotees who had come up from the city for the afternoon. Baba did not see them immediately since Vivek had hung back and sat hidden behind one of the marble pillars at the end of the pavilion, near the inner sanctum. Baba was replying to a middle-aged devotee who had asked how he could live in the world and still receive Divine grace.

'Associate the world mentally with God. Hold on to His feet with one hand and do your work with the other. Remember that all persons and things are His, not yours. Your father is Shiva, your mother Parvati, your son Krishna. A person who lives in a constant spiritual mood which makes him see that everything is part of God, *is* God, and he loses the fear of death. Such a person is rare. What did Hanuman answer when Rama asked, "How do you look at me?"

'"O Rama, as long as I have the feeling of 'I', I see that Thou art the whole and I am a part; Thou art the master and I am Thy servant. But, O Rama, when I have the knowledge of Truth, I realize that Thou art I and I am Thou."'

At the end, the discursive note had given way to an intimate one, as if he was now conversing with someone inside himself. The light in his eyes began to change, turned inward—a lamp switched on in a room where the curtains have been drawn. He stood up, staggering a little. Two young disciples sprang up to help but Baba shrugged off their support and began to walk towards the inner sanctum. The squatting men shifted on the floor to give way, touching their foreheads to the ground in deep reverence as he walked past them.

'Just look at his face! He is entering samadhi!' awed voices whispered to each other.

As the door of the inner sanctum closed behind him, Vivek turned toward Kamal in obvious agitation.

'The foolishness of it all! How can a created being consider himself the Creator? I am God, you are God. What could be more absurd? This pillar is God, all that I see is God, we are all God . . .'

He began to laugh. Heads turned, sharply disapproving of the unseeming levity. From inside the sanctum, Baba must have heard Vivek. They did not see him till he was standing next to them. He was smiling, but his eyes were half-closed and he did not seem to be fully conscious.

'What were you two talking about?' he said, and put his hands on Vivek's shoulder. Instantly, Vivek felt everything within him and outside begin to change, as if the earth had jumped into another orbit. There was no frightening sensation of disintegration like the one he had experienced before, only the deep conviction that he and the world around him were irrevocably transformed. His consciousness seemed to split in two: one familiar, possessing a continuity from when he was a child, and the other a complete stranger—the unknown more vivid and clearly defined than the known. It was as if two movies were being simultaneously screened in his mind. Both had the same actors and identical scenes. But the director of one was mediocre, his work drearily familiar, whereas the other movie was a revelation, a surpassing world of art conceived by a genius. In the opening scene of the first movie, Vivek was returning home, cycling down Purana Ghat, listening to Kamal talk about their afternoon visit but not offering any comments of his own. In the other, Vivek was still cycling down Purana Ghat with Kamal at his side, but everything around him—the *chhatris*, the garden houses, the cycle-rickshaws and the trucks, the people walking on the road—was bathed in a wondrous light that connected him and all that he saw in some profound way. In his inner ear, he heard an indescribably sweet voice, neither recognizably male nor female, sing the thought that would not leave him: 'Nothing exists but God!'

The movies would not stop. He tried to collapse them into one, return to the familiar contents of his consciousness before the incursion, but was powerless to stop what was happening. When he reached home, he sat down to eat. He put a few morsels of rice in his mouth and then stopped.

'Why are you sitting still? Eat!' he heard his mother say.

He could not taste the food. He felt it was someone else eating. There was no sensation in his tongue or in his limbs. He wondered if his body was paralyzed, even though he felt as light as air.

'I am going out,' he said.

Turning right on Bhagwan Das Road, Vivek started walking towards Statue Circle. At some point of time, he must have left the pavement and walked onto the road, for he heard car horns blaring angrily. In one version of the movie, he wanted to step back to the safety of the pavement. In the other, he felt deeply connected with the playful vehicles swerving around him.

Arriving at Statue Circle, Vivek sat down on a stone bench next to the ice cream man with his wooden pushcart and his standard offering of three flavours: vanilla, chocolate and strawberry. Two small children, a boy and a girl, came laughing up to the cart. He watched them bear away a stick of chocolate ice cream in triumph to their parents who were squatting on the grass next to the canopy under which Sawai Man Singh's statue was still to be installed. As the ice cream was passed around, each family member giving it a long, slurping lick, Vivek felt its chill numb his own tongue and slowly creep down his gullet. He looked down at the bench. It seemed so insubstantial, almost chimerical, that he could not understand how it could support his weight. He rapped his knuckles sharply on the stone to see if the bench was real. The sudden shock of a sharp pain shooting up his arm stopped the second movie for a few moments before the projector whirred back to life and it restarted. It took three days—and nights, each with its two sets of concurrent dreams—before the other consciousness withdrew and Vivek returned to his normal state.

It would be wrong to conclude that because of these experiences Vivek was suddenly transformed from a sceptic to some kind of a believer and accepted Baba as a spiritual guide with an access to the Divine. The experiences were indeed vital, but for a long time their meaning remained obscure. They shook, perhaps even rearranged the furniture of his mind but seemed to drain away in myriad small channels before they could rise to the surface of his consciousness. There were certain changes, yes, but these were more at the level of unreflective action than deeply-held convictions. He spoke to no one about his experiences. The little time he spent at home during the day, he shut himself in his father's study. Here he slept or skimmed through Trilok Nath's books, ignoring his mother's reproachful looks whenever she came in to ask if he needed anything. He became disinterested in food. Whatever was given to him, tasty or insipid, less or more, he swallowed with the same indifference. He began to visit the Sitaram temple with some regularity. Here, he listened to Baba talk of God and answer questions from the devotees and even the occasional cynic without feeling indignant at what was being said. He saw Baba fall into trance-like states, wherein he would sing and dance before he lost complete consciousness, without feeling repelled. He no longer experienced the sadhu's laugh as the manic hilarity of a madman but resonated to its underlying gravity. Its effect on him was what he imagined Buddha's smile must have had on his disciples, nudging them towards compassion for human folly and life's absurdities. He smiled now when Baba laughed, but was not yet carried away to break into a laughter of his own.

Vivek struggled all the way against accepting Baba as his guru. His struggle, of course, was also against the betrayal of an adored and idealized father and all that he had stood for.

'I have nothing against the guru of Vedic times who was a guide to the correct performance of ritual and an instructor in religious duties,' he could hear his father speak, the amateur historian coming into his element. 'I even approve of the guru of the Upanishads, a teacher of acute intellect who demanded from the disciple the exercise of his reason and power of discrimination. What I dislike is this modern equation of the guru with God and all the nauseating emotionalism and blind obedience this equation entails. I have seen bold men become mooning women in their surrender to the guru. They long to see him, hear him, touch him. They put the dust of his feet on their head and drink the water in which he has washed his dusty, if not dirty, feet. I cannot understand how a human being can voluntarily subject himself to another in such abject fashion. This guru business has been a curse on Indian manliness.'

Baba, on the other hand, could not praise the virtues of complete and wilful surrender enough. At such times Vivek had the feeling that he was being directly addressed.

'When you surrender to the guru, you become a vacuum, an abyss, a bottomless pit. Then the guru begins to manifest himself in you. His energy begins to flow into you. You have to surrender your Self till you become a part of the guru. You hear with the guru's ears, see with the guru's eyes, taste with the guru's tongue, feel with the guru's skin. Arjuna had that kind of devotion. One day while riding with Arjuna in a chariot, Lord Krishna looked at the sky and said, "See, friend, how beautiful is that flock of pigeons!"

'Arjuna looked up and said, "Yes, Lord, very beautiful pigeons indeed."

'The very next moment Krishna looked again and said, "How strange, friend, these are not pigeons at all. They are geese."

'Arjuna saw the birds and said, "Quite so, they are geese."

'Now try and understand. Arjuna's truthfulness was legendary. He would never have flattered Krishna. But he had such great faith in Krishna's words, his surrender was so complete, that he actually saw with his eyes whatever Krishna described, true or false.'

He then pointed to Vivek, his broad smile overflowing with affection, and said to the young disciples who had been listening raptly, 'This one has the nature of a lion. He will not surrender easily. But once a lion is tamed, he becomes the mount for the Goddess Durga. Their combined spiritual power is awesome, capable of vanquishing the most powerful of demons.'

Chapter Fifteen

Vivek now spent all his evenings at the Sitaram temple, drawn by the strange power that Baba had on him, and anxious also to be away from the dingy and airless rooms that the family had rented above a sweets shop in Gopalji ka Rasta. The unending din of bicycle bells, radios blaring film songs, the cries of hawkers, and the curses of tonga drivers nudging their scabrous horses through the crowds that spilled over from the pavements made him feel more and more irritable as the day wore on. He could not get used to the stench from the open gutter flowing along the alley which, mixed with the sickly caramel-and-milk smells from the sweet shop, wafted all day long into the room that he shared with his mother.

The area where they had lived earlier, the C-Scheme, built up in the forties but greatly expanded since Independence, lay outside the old city walls. It was now home to cabinet ministers, civil servants and high court judges, and to the barons of old Jaipur state who had built stately mansions for their frequent stays in the capital. The move to the other side of the walls, to the bazaars of old Jaipur, was hardly a couple of miles in geographical distance but immense in cultural space. It was a move back across the divide that separated rulers from subjects, the aspirationally modern from the determinedly traditional, the confident future from an anxious past. It was a rude awakening from the dream that Trilok Nath had dreamt for himself and his family. It was, in fact, the ultimate nightmare of the Indian middle class: drowning in the surrounding ocean of poverty which had been kept at bay by large bungalows, well tended gardens and wide roads lined with bougainvillea and jacaranda trees. The grant of a small monthly pension by the Maharaja which had come through a few days before they moved to Gopalji ka Rasta had helped stem the panic but was not enough to banish the spectre of destitution for ever.

Vivek usually cycled to Sitaram temple after dusk when most of the visitors and devotees had left and Baba sat outside his room in relaxed conversation with his young disciples. Even in winter, Baba would take off the cloth in which he wrapped himself during the day and sit on the bare ground, naked because he often forgot to put on his loincloth. Once he proudly told his disciples that he had learnt to be careful about his clothes and never went about naked as before. When the boys began to laugh, Baba looked at himself to discover that he was sitting there stark naked, his loincloth folded under his arm. 'I can never improve!' the embarrassed saint exclaimed, 'I just can't remember to wear clothes.'

'But Baba, you are a Paramahamsa,' Vivek said, teasing him, careful not to let the tenderness he felt stray into his voice. 'Remember? You yourself told us the identifying signs of a Paramahamsa: the gait of a child, a face suffused with mirth, eyes swimming in joy, body completely unaware of itself, of whether it is naked or clothed.'

Baba brightened visibly.

'I still wish I could remember, though,' he said.

During the evenings, Baba kept the boys amused with a succession of stories and sermons and awed with his frequent samadhis. Then there was singing. Above all, singing. Baba would take the lead in songs of praise or longing for the Lord, the young disciples enthusiastically joining in the refrain while one of them provided music with drums or cymbals. Sometimes, moved by deep emotion, Baba would stand up and begin to dance with a jerky grace, and the disciples would dance around him in a circle. Baba's dancing invariably culminated in the ecstatic trance of bhava samadhi: eyes half closed and his face lit up in a beatific smile, his body would suddenly become rigid and he would begin to sway unsteadily on his feet. When the dancing stopped one of the young men had to support him at the elbow till his normal consciousness gradually returned. Later, they would all sit down together to eat a simple meal, generally coarse-grained rice with a seasonal vegetable and dal. Baba personally distributed the food on banana leaves, often feeding one or the other disciple with his own hands, presiding over his extended family of half-a-dozen youths like a fussy but loving mother.

Partly due to feelings of shame at his reduced circumstances, Vivek's contact with his friends was now almost nonexistent. Kamal was the only one who still sought him out at college and tried to draw him back from what he felt was a disastrous descent into superstition, magic and irrationality. One afternoon, after classes were over, Vivek was sitting in the canteen with books he had just borrowed from the library piled on the table in front of him. Kamal had come up to him and picking up the books one by one, riffled impatiently through the pages. The books were about mystics and mysticism, an eclectic introduction to the world of saints and Sufis, the teachings of Tao and Zen, the trances of Teresa and Ramakrishna. Kamal was aghast.

'Is this where you hide these days? In this world of illusion and rampant subjectivity? Is your philosophy finally going to culminate in a study of the private madnesses of crazed people?'

'Why call their experiences private? Any one willing to go through the required spiritual training can expect the same results. After all, scientific knowledge is also not available to everyone but only to those trained in the sciences, and yet no one doubts that it is public.'

Kamal was incensed.

'So your Baba is at the same level as Einstein? Listen, his trances and loss of consciousness are not experiments giving special insights into nature but symptoms of a nervous disorder. Hysteria perhaps, or even epilepsy. Einstein!'

Vivek smiled. He remembered a recent evening when Baba had asked, 'You study philosophy, don't you? Tell me, what is this thing called logic?'

'Well, Baba, there are two kinds of logic: deductive and inductive,' Vivek had replied. 'The first is a method of reasoning that progresses from the general to the particular. For example: All men are mortal. Scholars are men. Therefore scholars are mortal. The second method reasons from the particular to the general. For example . . .'

Baba was already bored. 'Is this what you get out of your books? What good are they? The almanac makes a forecast of the rainfall for the year but you won't get a drop of water by squeezing it. You are born to bathe in the ocean of Divine love. Not to gather knowledge from books. You have come to the orchard to eat mangoes. What is the need to know how many thousands of branches and millions of leaves there are in the orchard? Each moment I pray to God, "O Rama, give me enough knowledge to chant your name. That is all the knowledge I need."'

'What is important then, Baba?' a disciple had asked.

'What is important is to stop asking questions,' Baba had said with a gentle smile.

Yes, Baba can be compared to Einstein, Vivek wanted to tell Kamal. He is the great physicist's opposite. Einstein never wanted us to stop asking questions.

'And then,' Kamal was saying, 'the man cannot decide if he is a man or a woman! A sage who is a *hijra*—a saint in drag!'

Vivek tried hard to control his outrage.

'I have learnt from Baba that femininity in a man is a mark of high spirituality. He says that to feel towards the Lord as a woman feels towards the beloved man, open and receptive, anxious and sick with longing when he is away, imbues a devotee's prayer with that essential feeling without which the Lord does not reveal himself.'

'Oh, come on, *yaar*,' Kamal snapped. 'You believe all that rubbish? His problem is not spiritual but biological. The man even has breasts like those of a woman.'

'So what?' Vivek retorted. 'Ramakrishna, the saint of Dakshineshwar—he too grew breasts when he was a boy, although modern doctors call it a medical condition. Just as they dismiss his menstruating as a case of haemorrhoidal bleeding. The doctors do not know that in the evolved person the barrier between male and female is as thin as rice paper. Baba says that the bodies of saints do not blindly follow the biological plan laid out for them. The spirit's striving alters the sluggish fatalism of the body, encroaching even upon that last bastion of gender—the genitals. There is at least one modern saint, regarded as God by his devotees all over the world, who was not born a true hermaphrodite but has become one. Such matters generally remain secret.'

He gathered his books, preparing to leave. Kamal felt he had gone too far.

'All right, forget all this,' he said. 'At least have a cup of tea before you go. We used to have such good times together. Who knows when we shall meet again. I am off to America after the exams, I have a scholarship from the University of Illinois. No dusky tea-pickers in Assam for me.'

On the same evening, to Vivek's great surprise, Baba inquired about Kamal, something he had never done earlier.

'Where is your friend who came here with you? Why doesn't he come anymore?'

He was sitting on the parapet of the well, the boys squatting on the grass in front of him. It was a mild evening, unusual for the middle of February when cold winds, heavy with desert sand, whip through the plains of Rajasthan, peppering the face and chilling the bones. In the veranda of the hut, a large pot of red lentils was simmering over a coal fire.

Vivek repeated the afternoon's conversation in the college canteen. For the first time, he saw Baba become agitated.

'He calls my condition a disease? And all these people who day and night think only about money are normal? So those who dream of buying mansions and riding in new cars are sober and fully aware. And I, who only think of Him whose consciousness pervades the entire universe am supposed to be suffering from a disease which makes my mind unconscious! In their world, even a man who believes he can fulfil his obligations to his mother by offering to pay rent for the nine months he spent in her womb will be regarded as sane, whereas I who seek to dwell with God am mad.'

Still unwilling to commit himself to one or the other side, Vivek tried to defend his friend.

'Baba, most educated people think this way. I myself doubt your visions of gods and goddesses.'

'Why do you come here, then?'

'Because I love you,' Vivek blurted out before he had time to reflect upon an answer.

Baba walked up to Vivek and took him in his arms, his stubbly cheek resting lightly on the boy's broad shoulder.

'You have made me very happy today,' he said through his tears that soon soaked through Vivek's shirt.

Baba was unusually animated that evening. His eyes sparkled and his hands danced as he encouraged the young men gathered around him to ask questions. While he talked, his eyes often returned to Vivek's face before, satisfied, they moved away in an arc to take in the adoring faces raised toward him like the petals of a morning glory opening to the sun. Each disciple felt as if Baba's eyes engaged his alone, that he was being seen in the minutest detail as in a clear mirror, receiving a secret ray of love meant only for him.

'How does one deal with people like Vivek's friend who are dear to you but scoff at your spiritual side?' Raj Singh, the youth from the wrestling gymnasium, asked.

'Ignore them. Worldly people say all kinds of things about the spiritually minded. But look, when an elephant passes by, any number of dogs bark but the elephant pays them no attention. Among the doubters there may be a few highly evolved beings who are struggling against their own spiritual nature. They are temporarily ignorant, not wicked.'

He looked meaningfully at Vivek.

'But what about the wicked? Should one ignore someone who is intent on harming you?'

'With the truly wicked it is different. To live in the world you have to protect yourself from them, even with a show of violence. But you must not harm any one in anticipation of an injury. Let me tell you a story.

'There were once some cowherds who grazed their cattle in a meadow which was home to a very poisonous snake. One day a sadhu was about to walk through the meadow when the boys ran up to him and warned him about the snake.

'"Don't worry, children," the sadhu said. "I know a mantra which will make the snake quite harmless."

'When the sadhu came to the middle of the meadow, the snake rushed towards him, its hood raised threateningly. The sadhu chanted the mantra and the snake lay at his feet, weak as an earthworm.

'"Look here," the sadhu said, "Why do you go around harming others? You should be ashamed of yourself. I shall initiate you into the spiritual life. You will be rid of your violent nature and ultimately realize God."

'The snake bowed in acquiescence, was given a monastic name and initiated into the spiritual life.

'Soon the cowherds noticed that the snake was no longer dangerous. Each day, it lay peacefully in the sun, chanting God's name. They threw stones at it. It showed no anger, just slithered away to escape its tormentors. One day, one of the more daring boys came nearer, caught the snake by its tail, whirled it around and then dashed it against the ground. The snake was badly injured but finally succeeded in dragging itself into the safety of its hole. While it recovered, it rarely ventured out for fear of the cowherds, barely surviving on leaves and rotten fruit that dropped from the trees.

'A year later, the sadhu came that way again and asked the cowherds about the snake. "We have not seen it for a long time," the boys replied. "Perhaps it is dead." The sadhu did not believe them and went around the meadow, calling the snake by the monastic name he had given it at the time of initiation. The snake, weak from hunger and slowly recovering from its wounds, finally appeared.

'"What has happened to you?" the sadhu asked.

'The snake narrated the story of its travails and then added:

'"The boys are ignorant, after all. No blame attaches to them. They did not realize that I had changed. How were

they to know that I will never bite or harm anyone ever
again?"

'The sadhu was incensed.

'"You are a fool! You don't know how to protect
yourself. I asked you not to bite but you could have at least
hissed and scared them away."

'Therefore, remember: one should not bite the wicked
but there is no harm in hissing.'

The disciples laughed and Baba beamed with pleasure.

'But Baba, must one become a monk and renounce the
world? Is there no help for the worldly person?' Vivek asked

'Certainly there is. If he can only realize that his soul is
bound. That he is enslaved by the world, tied to it by fetters
of lust and greed. From time to time he should seek solitude
and pray for faith and devotion. There is nothing greater
than faith. Rama, who is God, had to build a bridge across
the sea to reach Lanka. But Hanuman, trusting only in
Rama's name, cleared the sea in one jump.

'Of course, the faith must be in an outside power, not in
one's own self. Once a disciple who had firm faith in his guru
came to a river. Closing his eyes and simply uttering the name
of the guru he crossed the river by walking on water. Seeing
this, the guru thought, "If my mere name has such power
then how great I myself must be!" The next day, the guru also
tried to walk across the river, uttering, "I, I, I." He sank.

'Faith in your own self binds you to the world even more
than lust or greed. The mind is nothing but a bundle of
thoughts and the first and foremost among them is the primal
"I" thought. All spiritual disciplines seek to annihilate the
"I" thought. The road to freedom, to salvation, lies through

the elimination of "I", never through its reinforcement.'

As he spent more and more time with Baba, Vivek felt he had begun to comprehend the nature of his fascination with this strange man. The fascination may have had its origins in the baffling sensations and odd perceptions he had experienced when Baba had first touched him, shattering the prism through which he had been accustomed to viewing himself in the world. But his mind had hastened to erase those particular memories, reconstructing the prism so well that the cracks where the fragments had been cemented together were visible only in an occasional nightmare. What now enthralled him was Baba's effortless transcendence of categories that he had been taught to view as opposites. In Baba, he beheld the easy coexistence of the child and the sage, of intense emotional outpouring and abstruse thought. And the totally contrasting states of being followed each other with a rapidity that verged on the simultaneous. Baba could laugh, sing, dance, cry tears of devotional joy or longing, enter an ecstatic trance or wax eloquent on the interconnectedness of spirit and flesh, body and mind, human and Divine—all within the space of a few minutes. After his years of training in western philosophy which had emphasized closely reasoned argument as the only mode of inquiry into the nature of reality, Vivek found it both disconcerting and exhilarating to discover someone like Baba for whom stories constituted a perfectly adequate guide to the structure of reality. He had never met someone quite like him who used the story as a way of thinking, a way of reasoning about complex situations.

Thus Vivek began to understand his fascination with

Baba, but what still puzzled him was Baba's attraction to him. Of all the young men who called themselves his disciples, Vivek, who till the very end struggled against identifying himself as one, was Baba's undisputed favourite. Indeed, Baba's infatuation with Vivek grew by the day. In full view of his disciples and devotees and the casual visitors who now came to the temple in droves, attracted by Baba's increasing renown, Baba would caress Vivek's face, constantly seek to touch his body and, to the boy's discomfiture, stare intently at him for long stretches of time. Baba's intense need for physical closeness, for the welcome touch of other bodies, was not limited to Vivek. Ajay, the youngest of the group, a fourteen-year-old boy whose feelings towards Baba were those of a child toward his mother, often lay curled on the ground with his head on Baba's lap, even when Baba was meditating or giving a discourse. On more than one occasion, Vivek had seen Baba, possessed by the mood of Yashoda, Krishna's mother, offer Ajay his fleshy breast, and the boy suckled at it with every sign of satisfaction. Another time, Baba had asked Raj Singh to wrestle with him.

'He is such a little man,' Raj Singh later narrated, 'and I am big and strong. So I pinned him down easily. His body was soft and delicate, just like a baby's. But I felt a surge of energy pour into me through the physical contact.'

Even when Vivek argued with Baba—he was the only one to do so, to the obvious discomfort of other disciples—the older man was never affronted. He admired the young man's spirited resistance as an expression of his lion-like nature. One evening the discussion had turned to marriage—Raj Singh's parents were exerting pressure on the boy for an early marriage.

'Bricks and tiles, if burnt after the mark of the brick factory has been stamped on them, retain these marks forever. But parents marry their children much too early these days. They are unmarked, open to any impression. And marriage is the root of bondage. It sets free the forces of lust, greed and avarice. The priests of the temple of Govindji were celibates once and possessed a fiery, spirited nature. Once, when the Maharaja of Jaipur sent for them, they haughtily said to the messenger that the king should come to them. The king was perturbed by their fierce nature. So he consulted a wise minister, who asked the king to get the priests to marry. The king did so. After that, the king never needed to send for the priests. They would appear by themselves, bringing offerings from the temple and wanting money—to build a house, for the naming ceremony of a child, to help with the school fees, to spend on the wedding of the wife's sister.'

'Is marriage against God's will?' Vivek protested. 'How will creation go on if men and women cease to marry?'

Baba regarded him with fondness.

'Don't worry about that. Let God worry about His creation. Those who like to marry are at perfect liberty to do so. I say what I must. You may accept as much or as little as you like.'

For almost three weeks in March, Vivek did not visit the temple. His final examinations were to begin in April and in spite of his indifference to his studies, he had decided to sit for them. A university degree was essential for even the lowest-paid white-collar job and although his worries about

the family's financial situation had lessened, they were by no
means over. Baba intuitively sensed whenever Vivek was
preoccupied by his financial difficulties. One evening it was
raining, a freak late-February shower, and the disciples were
huddled together in Baba's small room. At Baba's urging,
Vivek had begun to sing when Baba abruptly stood up and
left the room. Vivek stopped singing and the young men
looked at each other in bewilderment. After a few minutes,
Baba returned, drops of water dripping down his head, and
loudly announced:

'I listened to his singing but didn't enjoy it at all. So I left
the room. His mind is on earning money and therefore his
song sounded dull, like curry without salt.'

For a long time Vivek remained unaware of the strength
of Baba's obsession with him. He did not know that his
absence could cause Baba extreme torment till Raj Singh
landed up at his house early one morning, even before Vivek
had bathed, to relate the happenings of the previous day at
the temple. Baba had been distracted the whole afternoon.
His answers to the devotees' questions were desultory,
lacking the endearing spontaneity that normally animated
his speech. In the evening, too, when the disciples gathered
around him on the veranda in front of the hut, Baba did not
join in the kirtan and his clapping to the beat of the songs was
half-hearted at best. Dinner was early and subdued. Baba did
not eat at all. After most of the disciples left, Baba asked Raj
Singh and Ajay who were spending the night with him
whether they preferred to sleep in his room or outside on the
veranda. Raj Singh thought their presence inside the hut
could disturb Baba's early morning meditation and opted for

the veranda. The boys had been asleep for a while, curled up in their quilts, when they were startled awake by a strangled cry. Baba was coming out of his room, reeling like a drunkard, his loincloth clutched in his right fist.

'Are you asleep?' he asked.

'No, Baba.'

'Will you please tell Vivek to come? Can you bring him here? I feel as if someone is wringing my heart, squeezing out all the blood—like this,' he said, twisting the loincloth with both his hands. Even in the dim light of the crescent moon peering through the thinning clouds, Raj Singh could see the agonized expression on his guru's face. Baba then turned and walked a few steps back into his room before he returned.

'Don't forget to tell him. Promise you will remember.'

An hour later, he woke up the boys again.

'Look here, he is very pure. I view him as an incarnation of Krishna and cannot live without him. His absence is wringing my heart like this.' He again twisted the cloth. Then, in a voice choking with anguish said, 'Let him come here. Just once. I must see him.'

The scene was repeated thrice during the night.

When Vivek cycled up to the temple later that afternoon, he was ill-prepared for the extraordinary reception that awaited him. Baba was sitting with the disciples and devotees on the marble floor of the temple pavilion, telling a story in answer to a question one of them had asked. As soon he saw Vivek, he broke off in mid-sentence.

'There is Vi . . . There is Vi . . .!' he cried out, his voice snapping with emotion, unable to complete Vivek's name. His fluttering hands and beseeching eyes urgently summoned the boy to sit next to him. His eyes were brimming with tears as he furiously caressed Vivek's face, like a blind mother seeking to rediscover and engrave in her memory the features of a son who had returned home after a long absence and who may suddenly disappear again. He then took Vivek's feet onto his lap and gently began to massage the insteps and the soles. Oblivious to the presence of others, he asked Vivek to sing while he continued to gaze at the embarrassed boy's face in utter adoration. With an apologetic shrug of his shoulders, Vivek complied:

> *Tell me friend, how far the grove*
> *Where my beloved Krishna dwells.*
> *His fragrance reaches me even here*
> *But I am tired and can walk no further.*

Baba was drifting off into ecstasy even as Vivek sang. His eyelids were drooping, the pupils turning up. The gliding motion of his hands on Vivek's feet came to a halt. Suddenly, he got up, stood on his toes, his sightless eyes peering through the curtain that hides the play of gods from mortal eyes, and from deep within his chest, came an ecstatic shout:

'Watch out, Radha! You crazy girl, mad with Krishna's love, you will fall into the Yamuna!'

He tottered on his spindly legs and then abruptly sat down in Vivek's lap.

'I was testing how much weight you can bear,' he said when normal consciousness had returned.

Later, when the disciples were leaving after finishing the evening meal, Baba asked Vivek to stay back. It had been a long day and of late Baba seemed to tire easily. But he did not want to go to bed and refused Vivek's offer of a massage for his aching feet. As they sat outside the hut under the quiet stars, the night becoming stiller as one by one the evening sounds disappeared into a well of silence, Baba began to talk.

'You remember the first time you came, and I recognized you at once?'

Vivek nodded. How could he ever forget the day his father died!

'A week before you came, the Lord commanded me in a vision, "Share your love of the Divine with a human being. Love another person as you love Me." Ah, it was a strange and wondrous vision! For when the Lord receded you appeared in his place, a small boy who was crying for his mother. When I returned to the world my nipples were aching, as if my breasts were heavy with milk.'

Vivek was listening intently, no longer an automatic scoffer of matters which did not fit neat philosophical categories.

'Have you still not understood? In you is the male principle and in me the female. You are Rama and I am Sita and these two have always, always been One.'

On the same night, as if in answer to Baba's vision, Vivek dreamt that Baba was standing at the bottom of a hill, beckoning to him. 'Come, I will show you the mother of the universe, the Goddess herself.' Vivek began to climb up the narrow winding path behind Baba, when Baba suddenly turned and Vivek saw that he was transformed into an exquisitely beautiful woman. She was smiling as she spread out her arms.

'You may rest now,' the woman said. 'You have arrived at your destination.'

Vivek awoke from the dream with an inexpressible feeling of peace that irradiated his body and had seeped into the deepest layers of his mind, bringing to a halt the restless succession of images, thoughts, sensations and feelings that colonize the waking mind. For an instant, he had gone beyond the mind to the other side of his being. Although the exact opposite of the terror and the sense of disintegration that he had experienced when Baba placed his foot in his lap, Vivek knew that this ineffable peace was connected to what had happened on that day. It was all part of a gift from Baba which he could now accept without needing to understand.

Like the stars turning pale with the approach of dawn, the dream soon dissipated, the morning sun sending its shadows scurrying away. But, again like the stars, the dream did not disappear; it only became invisible.

Chapter Sixteen

It was Indira Gandhi who made him famous.

This was in the spring of 1966. Indira Gandhi had come to Jaipur for a session of the All India Congress Committee six weeks after becoming the Prime Minister. Here, someone told her about Ram Das Baba and his visionary trances. Unlike Jawaharlal Nehru, her agnostic father who was more enamoured of Marxist than Hindu idols, Indira Gandhi was attracted by the spiritual side of life. Later, as her personality hardened, her nascent spirituality was debased by superstition and occultism; she consulted astrologers and soothsayers and is reputed to have carried out rites of propitiation and performed special prayers for political and personal purposes. In early 1966, though, when she came to Jaipur, she was intrigued enough by the tales she had heard about the ecstatic mystic to ask the Chief Minister of Rajasthan to arrange a private visit to the Sitaram temple.

Baba was sitting with his disciples when Indira Gandhi, accompanied only by her social secretary, another woman, entered the garden early in the evening. The rest of her retinue, including her security detail, was left outside. Familiar only to readers of newspapers, her face was not as

instantly recognizable then as it was to become in the next
twelve years of her imperious rule. Her head covered by the
pallu of her sari, she walked up to Baba with a firm stride and
bowed as if to touch his feet. And then something very
peculiar happened. Baba stumbled back as if stung by a
wasp. Turning his back on her, he rushed into his room.
Displaying an iron control over her emotions for which she
was later justly famous, Indira Gandhi smiled wanly at the
disciples, nodded to her secretary and walked out of
Dhamani's garden with measured, dignified strides.

The news of the Prime Minister's visit, though not its
details, was picked up by the local *Rajasthan Patrika* and
then found its way as a short item on the inside pages of
national dailies. It had the effect of sharply increasing the
number of visitors to the Sitaram temple just when Baba
seemed to be retreating from contact with the outside world.
In the last few weeks, Vivek had become aware of disquieting
changes in Baba's behaviour. Withdrawal, a definite turning
inwards, was one of them.

'I don't know why,' he had confided in Vivek, 'but the
sounds and colours of the world become dimmer with each
passing day. Everything outside seems to have been robbed
of all grace. Whatever I see with my eyes only reveals itself
when I see it again within.'

Baba was still vibrantly alive when he sang and danced
with the disciples but these occasions were now intermittent.
With strangers, he was increasingly silent. He made no effort
to shape his thoughts into words and was less inclined to
spontaneously give of himself to visitors. Often he did not
appear at the temple in the afternoons, to the great

disappointment of the devotees gathered there for his darshan. Many evenings with the disciples were curtailed when he would abruptly disappear into his room, cutting short the singing and dancing just when they had begun to take hold. The devotees and the disciples naturally put the most positive gloss on Baba's withdrawal, interpreting it 'upwards' in the time-honoured fashion of all believers. He was becoming like the ancient sages who never left their caves once they retired there for meditation, they said. He was like Rabiya, the famous Sufi saint who closed her shutters in springtime lest the beauty of flowers distract her from contemplating the beauty of her Beloved.

Baba's increasing withdrawal from the world also coincided with an abrupt turning away from women devotees. The incident with Indira Gandhi was not an aberration. Vivek had observed that Baba was uneasy in the afternoon meetings when young women were also present. He would hastily withdraw his feet if one of them tried to touch them in reverence. If a woman did succeed, Baba recoiled as if from an electric shock, his loss of composure evident. Once, while in the middle of a discourse, a young woman threw herself at his feet, catching him by surprise. Clutching his legs, she wept tears of devotion while he struggled to break free. Later, the disciples were astonished to see that there were large blisters at the back of Baba's legs where the woman had held him.

'I have become terribly scared of impure women,' he said to them. 'I see them as tigresses coming to devour me. It is with great difficulty that I can train my mind to see them as manifestations of the blissful Mother. All of you who are young and just starting on the spiritual path, remember that without chastity there can be no progress. Without it, you cannot even understand my discourses. Don't let yourself be ensnared by a woman's beauty. What is inside her anyway but entrails, piss, shit, phlegm!'

The news of the blisters had spread quickly, further adding to his reputation for holiness.

Vivek was bewildered. How could someone who had realized the underlying Self which is common to all sentient beings make a distinction between man and woman? Could even Baba fall prey to the illusion of outer appearance, be misled by the mere presence of breasts and vulva in a human being? He was no orthodox Brahmin preoccupied with matters of ritual purity who believed that women were inherently polluted through their intimate connection with the organic processes of life, especially menstruation and child birth. No, the only possible explanation for Baba's apparent misogyny lay in his withdrawal from the world in pursuit of unknown spiritual aims. If he was avoiding contamination by the world, Vivek reasoned, then he would naturally also avoid women through whom the world is renewed and perpetuated.

After writing his BA exams in April, Vivek now spent all his days and some of his nights at the garden. At Baba's urging, Dhamani's younger brother, who had promised the jeweller on his deathbed that he would look after 'father', had built a two-room stone hut in an abandoned corner of the garden after having it cleared of a thick bush of prickly pear. The rooms were available to any of the disciples who wished to stay for the night. The hut became a second home to Vivek. Even when he did not stay over at the hut, Vivek returned at daybreak and spent most of his mornings looking after the garden—clearing it of weeds, sweeping away the fallen leaves—and tending to a newly planted kitchen garden. At home, he and his family had little to say to each other. If his mother still hoped that he would one day look for a job and start a family, she was careful not to show it. Even though she had had to take a part-time position at the Maharani Gayatri Devi Public School, looking after the younger girls during the recess —'a glorified *ayah*', according to Sharada Devi—she never complained to Vivek when he was at home, watching him eat with a quiet adoration that had remained undiminished. Both kept alive the pretense that things would change once his results were declared in July. His grand-aunt was the only one who did not pretend that a final break with the family would occur only if he donned the ochre robes of a sadhu. Whenever he was at home and within earshot, she would loudly curse her fate which had arranged her marriage in a family where the men made a habit of leaving their women.

On the morning in the first week of June when his results were declared—he had passed with a first division—Vivek cycled straight back to Dhamani's garden. Walking up to Baba who was alone in his room, he asked to be initiated into spiritual life. He was eager to receive the mantra that would guide his meditation and set him off on his quest. But Baba was oddly reluctant.

'I love you more than any of the others but the time for your meditation has not yet arrived,' he said.

'Why not?' Vivek insisted.

'Learning the technique of meditation is fruitless without first imbibing its spirit. You must wait.'

'How can I get the spirit?'

'You cannot. The spirit of meditation is surrender and one cannot will surrender. It either happens or it does not. All one can do is create conditions that facilitate surrender.'

'And how will I know when that happens?'

'Through revelation—an imperative that one hears in the heart. And,' he added kindly, '*I* will know. Till the time comes, develop the love of Lord and practice concentrating your mind. Concentration is the beginning of meditation.'

Disappointed, Vivek turned back to books. He had kept his library card after graduation although he was now on the verge of exhausting Maharaja College's small collection of books on mysticism. Baba poked fun at his search for answers in books but also felt proud of his persistence.

'A lion!' he would exclaim in delight whenever Vivek argued with him in front of the disciples.

Lately, though, it seemed he had begun to find Vivek's intellectual combativeness a strain.

A week after Indira Gandhi's visit, when Vivek had not yet rationalized and accepted Baba's observations on the desired attitude toward women, the evening talk had turned to celibacy. This time Vivek did not hold back.

'Baba, celibacy is not a precondition for the realization of God. Not everywhere, anyway. Many well-known Jewish and Sufi mystics were married. Indeed, they taught that if one has sexual intercourse with the knowledge that God is present in the woman, the act itself becomes a means for spiritual perfection. Even in our country, the Shaktas advocate a heroic stance toward women that involves sex.'

Baba looked plainly at unease as he ruminatively scratched his beard.

'I don't like all that,' he said shortly. 'My own attitude toward women is like that of a child toward his mother.'

Vivek did not let up.

'Even asceticism! Not everyone believes that asceticism is a required part of the spiritual baggage. Swami Vivekananda called it "fiendish". He claimed it was "better to laugh than pray". He himself ate extravagantly and smoked expensive cheroots and cigars.'

Vivek turned to address the other young men who were listening open-mouthed.

'I read that when Swamiji was in the United States one of his admirers said to him, "You are a queer sort of saint. You eat well, you drink well, you smoke all day, and you deprive yourself of nothing." And then there is this swami in Bombay . . .'

Something in the disciples' faces made him stop. He turned around to see that Baba was hurrying away towards the temple.

At such times Vivek missed his friend Kamal. He could not discuss what he was reading in the books and the confusion it caused him with any of Baba's disciples. They were simple youths from Jaipur's bazaars, with little education though with great faith. There was none among them with whom he could share his growing enthusiasm for the writings of Swami Vivekananda and Shri Aurobindo. For both these highly regarded modern mystics, spirituality was the accumulation of power rather than grace. Aurobindo's

daily record of his Yogic meditation in his Pondicherry
ashram minutely detailed his progress in acquiring powers:
of telepathy, extrasensory perception, and acting on people
and objects through will alone, of freedom from sickness and
all that can weigh down the body, mind or soul, whether it is
gravity or depression. Vivekananda had even felt that the
Hindu cultivation of devotional mysticism had decisively
weakened the land and sapped the energy of its people. India,
he wrote contemptuously, was populated by women and
eunuchs and it was his mission to make *men* out of them. His
ideal was not the singing, dancing child of God but the manly
amalgam of saint and warrior, the militant mystic. Perhaps
Vishnu Das, the mahant of Galta, had the right idea. Vivek
had heard that Vishnu Das was trying to organize the sadhus
to help forge a strong Hindu nation and revive India's
ancient glory. Vivek had even written to the mahant,
expressing his admiration for what he was trying to do. Baba
was a great saint but did he comprehend the needs of the
modern world? Did he understand that the spirit's quest may
be eternal but the right path changes with history?

One day, late in the morning, after he had finished
working in the garden and was washing himself at the well,
Baba came out of the hut after his morning meditation and
watched him bathe. He sat at the edge of the parapet, looking
troubled. He waited for Vivek to get dressed before he spoke.

'I see fewer and fewer visions in my samadhis these days.
I wonder if I am gradually losing my feminine nature.'

His voice was doleful, seeking consolation. But Vivek,
who sometimes felt uncomfortable with Baba's trances and
with the abandoned singing and dancing of his disciples, saw

in Baba's gloom only an opening to express his own enthusiasm for the male spirituality of Vivekananda and Aurobindo. Baba listened for a while before his eyes glazed over. Vivek's voice faltered and then trailed into silence. Baba did not look at Vivek as he began to speak, his gaze skimming the top of the temple's spire.

'They were great and learned Yogis. I am but an illiterate rustic. Who am I to doubt their teachings? But, son, I have seen Rama with the eyes of Sita.

'Krishna came to me when I was Radha. They blessed me with a revelation. The secret purpose of our sly Lord is to make everything leap with ecstasy within us. Remember that, always, even after you have forgotten me . . . as you one day will.'

'Never!' Vivek cried, hastening to assure both of them of his devotion.

At first Vivek thought the changes in Baba had to do with the arrival of his mother.

When they saw her, the two disciples sitting in the veranda of Baba's hut, guardians of his afternoon rest, tried to turn away the old and obviously ailing woman who was little more than a bag of bones wrapped in a dirty sari of indeterminate colour.

'There is no Gopal here, Mother,' one of the young men said. 'This is the abode of the great saint Baba Ram Das.'

'You may rest under that tree,' said the other disciple, moved by the woman's condition. She was exhausted and on the verge of collapse.

The astrologer's teenaged son who had accompanied Amba from Deogarh and carried a bundle of her few clothes on his head now intervened.

'Baba Ram Das *is* Gopal, her son.'

'There he is!' Amba cried as Baba came out of the room, blinking into the sunlight. 'I have come to stay, Gopal. I want to die in your arms. Even if you were to throw away my body on the road outside, I must end this life in your arms.'

Deeply moved, Baba walked up to her and tenderly stroked her head, brushing back straggling wisps of thinning, grey hair. Soon, mother and son were crying while they held each other, Amba crooning endearments from the time of his childhood through her tears.

The journey to Jaipur in the summer heat of May must have worsened her condition. In spite of the best medical attention Dhamani's brother could arrange, Amba's sickness could not be diagnosed, the disease progressing rapidly in the three weeks she was fated to live with her son. Baba looked after her himself, giving her a bath when she became too weak to wash herself, coaxing her to eat a little at mealtimes, sitting up through the night, after the disciples had left, to talk to her of old times at Deogarh.

On Thursday, the eleventh day of the bright half of the lunar month of Jyesth, it was obvious that Amba's end had come. Baba went to her room after his morning meditation, closed the door behind him and stayed with her the whole day. The disciples waited outside, joined by a few curious devotees. Baba came out after sunset, gave instructions for the preparation of the evening meal and went back into the room. After the meal was over, he asked them all to enter the room and chant the name of Rama. Amba lay on the floor with her eyes closed, her chest heaving and her breath coming out in loud gasps. There was no indication that the name of the Lord was reaching her inner ear. Impassive, Baba sat by her side, holding her hand. In her last hour, he laid his right hand on her heart and the left on her head, not to prolong her life as some of the devotees thought, but to quieten the mind.

It seemed to Vivek that his mother's death hastened the changes in Baba. The change was most visible in the body. A low inner fire was slowly melting away all excess fat. The skin on his face became thin and the sharp bones became prominent. His breasts shrank. His body became alarmingly thinner by the day, as if rushing headlong towards the state of becoming pure spirit.

His need for the bodily touch of the younger disciples increased. Baba had always enjoyed the company of boys. He could joke, laugh, sing and dance with them whereas he felt constrained to be more serious in the presence of older men. In recent weeks, this tendency had become more pronounced. He avidly sought the proximity of young disciples, and his body instinctively moved in a way that created a distance between him and the older devotees who thronged the temple during the day. In the afternoon assembly, Ajay now almost always lay curled in his lap, his eyes regarding the surrounding faces with the arrogant indifference of a baby held snugly against the mother's breast. Even while Baba talked to the devotees, his hand absently stroked the boy's face. When Baba walked from the hut to the temple or back at the end of the assembly, he always had his right arm draped around the shoulder of one of the boys. The disciples would jostle each other to get closer to Baba when he stood up, vying with each other for this singular mark of his favour.

It was only afterwards that Vivek understood Baba's need for physical intimacy with the boys as a hankering for warmth by a body whose tissues and cells were being touched by the frost of death. At the time, though, he tried to understand it as a part of spiritual life. He felt angry and distressed whenever he heard a rare visitor—almost always a college student—comment on the unseemliness of Baba's craving. He would want to rush up to the offender and explain that Baba was like the Sufi saints who were convinced that the benefit of keeping company with beardless youths is that they are newer, of more recent origin in the Lord than older men; and whatever is closer to its creation is more sacred and more abundantly the occasion of grace than what is farther removed.

In hindsight, Vivek recognized in the changes that took place in Baba's personality that summer the initial symptoms of his throat cancer. The body's despair manifested itself earlier than the signs of its physical decay; the misogyny, the barren trances, the search for warmth in the bodies of young boys, were prior to the loss of weight, the swelling in the throat and the difficulties in swallowing.

Looking back, some of Baba's words on those evenings

took on added meaning. Once, emerging from an aborted samadhi, Baba had plaintively remarked that his throat ached in unuttered praise. Another evening, when the singing and dancing had begun, Baba suddenly sat down, saying his breath was too short for the celebration. At the time, Vivek marvelled at the metaphors, little realizing that they were also concrete descriptions of his physical condition.

The cancer was only discovered when the intermittent pain in his throat became so acute that Baba could no longer take his mind off it. Reluctantly, he agreed to be taken to SMS Hospital for tests. By this time the cancer was far advanced and surgery was no longer an option. Yet, in spite of the frequent spasms of pain that distorted his features and brought tears to his eyes, and the difficulty in swallowing food which reduced his meals to a watery gruel, Baba remained cheerful.

As his condition worsened, even Ajay who had held on to the belief that one of these days Baba would miraculously get rid of the tumour began to give up hope. Whenever Ajay insisted that Baba pray to Rama to make the cancer disappear, Baba would merely smile and affectionately stroke the boy's cheek.

'Don't look sad,' he tried to console the disciples. 'The thought that you'll weep and grieve when I go makes it more difficult for me to leave this body. Otherwise I do not fear death. How could I? I have died many times in uniting with the Lord. The only difference is that this time I shall not return.'

The rains had failed that year and the summer was unbearably long. In the garden, hot winds had coated the trees with layers of fine dust. The unrelenting sun singed the grass and frizzled the leaves on even the hardiest bushes. The scorching heat and Baba's rare appearances at the temple had reduced the throng of visitors to a trickle and brought to an end the afternoon assemblies. Some intrepid devotees still came to the garden in the morning or after sunset, hoping for Baba's darshan, but the disciples had thrown up a protective wall around him to allow him long periods of undisturbed rest. Only the truly devout were allowed in and the merely curious were turned away.

In the final weeks of his illness, Baba insisted that Vivek meet him every day. Vivek would normally go to Baba's hut at dawn. Baba was awake by this time, the unpredictable flaring up of pain having radically curtailed his hours of sleep and meditation. Vivek found their conversations, to which he had little to contribute except murmured words of assent or reassurance, an odd mixture of lofty thought and obsessive rumination. When not in pain, Baba would view his approaching death with equanimity. One morning, when Baba was almost his old cheerful self, Vivek asked if he was afraid. Baba smiled.

'Why should I fear that my mind will disappear, dissolve into nothing? That I will no longer go on wishing my wishes, will stop thinking my thoughts? If you are not attached to your mind, have no pride in the contents of your consciousness, there is no fear.'

Ajay, who now spent all his days and nights with Baba, sleeping on the floor at the foot of Baba's cot, was waking up. Baba watched fondly as the boy stretched, yawned and rubbed away the dust of sleep from his eyes.

'Baba, would you like your legs to be massaged now or after I finish my bath?' Ajay asked, placing his hand gently on Baba's knee.

'Later,' Baba replied, his face softening as his body accepted the soothing touch.

'Of course, the body will not give up quietly,' he continued. 'Not because of fear but because it is in the body's nature to struggle against extinction. All I want is to go quickly, not linger on, forever taking leave.'

But when he was in pain, Baba's mind would hurtle down the incline of obsessive doubt. He had not repaid his debts, he worried. Had he not abandoned the mother who had given him life and, beyond that, a love that had wanted nothing for itself except the beloved son's proximity? How had he served Madhavacharya who had guided his first steps into the life of the spirit? By taking away his Ram-lalla! And Nangta, whom he had worshipped but finally betrayed by straying from the path the guru had charted for him? Vivek would listen, fidgeting on the stool next to the bed, wanting to shut his ears to the confessional flow. He found himself unable to offer comfort, the upsurge of love that made him want to throw his arms around Baba's shrunken frame blocked by an unease insisting on immediate flight.

Most of all, Baba worried about the disciples.

'For six months after I came here I was alone. I used to wander around in the garden, crying to Rama, "Where are my disciples? When will they come? I need them just like You need believers, O Lord."'

Even Baba cannot deny the claims of nature, Vivek thought. To have disciples is the only way ascetics and celibates can have families of their own.

'What will happen to them after I am gone?' Baba agonized. 'Will they stay together? They are young boys, easily tempted. Especially by women. Ajay is the only one whose soul is so pure that it is safe from the ravages of lust. Who will remind them of the precautions to be taken when a woman comes too close? Never let yourself feel the air from her body and keep yourself at least two cubits away from all women except your mother.'

In the last three days of his life, Baba was miraculously free of pain except when he wanted to drink water. At such times he winced sharply with every mouthful he tried to force down his lacerated throat, trying to appease a burning thirst that refused to disappear as quietly as had his hunger. On the last night, another full moon in the month of August, almost exactly sixteen years after Nangta had initiated Gopal at the same spot, Baba gave initiation to ten of his disciples who he hoped would build the nucleus of a future Ram Das Mission.

One by one, they entered the room where Baba lay on his rumpled cot, propped up against a thick bolster Raj Singh had brought for him. The initiations were brief, lasting but a few minutes. Each disciple's personal mantra was whispered into his ear. Baba spoke some words of instruction and blessing which were also those of farewell, and it was over. Yet the whole process took more than four hours since Baba's periods of rest between the initiations became longer as the night wore on.

It was daybreak when Vivek, who was the last to be

called, entered the room. Outside, the garden was awakening to the chatter of parrots, the summer light making a day out of dawn even before the sun had risen. The appearance of the Sun-god's chariot on the horizon, the impatient pawing of its horses, seemed to have infused Baba with a brief surge of fresh life. The movement of his beckoning hand was forceful and his voice vibrant as he asked Vivek to come and sit on the cot at his feet.

'Give me your hand,' he said.

For a few seconds he kept looking at Vivek's face, his eyes shining with love before they were again slowly clouded over by the sickness.

'You don't need a mantra or a formal initiation,' he said, his voice trembling with tenderness as much as by exhaustion. 'You have been already initiated by my touch. Remember? The first time I put my foot on your lap?'

He closed his eyes. His hands were warm although his breath was fetid, already marked by the body's hastening decay. Baba's small frame had shrunk further. His protruding shoulder blades and the ribcage were pushing hard against the papery grey skin. There were deep furrows in the cheeks, just above the line of his straggly beard. The circles under his eyes were like ink blots spreading under the skin. He shook his head when he opened his eyes, as if clearing a vision blurred by approaching death. His voice, though, was still strong.

'I have told the others. You will take my place. Take them along on whichever road you choose, my son.'

His anointment by Baba as his heir did not surprise Vivek this morning as it might have any other day. For this was a

singular morning on which the stars had not become pale
and then invisible but shone in all their nocturnal brightness.
He knew he loved Baba, intensely, fiercely, even as he was
baffled by this love. But he was no longer sure of the path his
own quest would take. Only the other day, he had received a
gracious letter from Vishnu Das in reply to his own, asking
him to visit Galta.

'Perhaps you will choose a path other than my own just
as I did with Nangta,' Baba was saying. 'Perhaps you are not
destined to know that desperate love for the Lord which
sends storms of rapturous feeling snaking through the body,
making the very marrow in your bones beat as wildly as your
pulse.'

Vivek looked up. Baba was gazing past him through the
half open door. Between the bed and the door, a small pool
of sunlight slowly spread on the floor. Baba's eyes were
turning up, peering beyond the dark curtain that falls at the
end of life into lighted spaces that Vivek would never see.

'The death of the body is not its victory, Vivek,' he was
whispering now.   'The body will go . . . but remember, the
soul will eternally cry delight.'

Baba's eyes closed. Soft snores with a faint but
unmistakable rattle at the end came from the direction of the
cot. Outside, a peacock welcomed the awakening of the
world and the birth of another day with a raucous cry.

Epilogue

After two years of working with Vishnu Das, during which he travelled all over north India with the mahant, visiting monasteries and helping to set up a network of sadhus committed to the creation of a united Hindu society, Vivek decided to become a full-time worker in the Rashtriya Swayamsevak Sangh, the core organization of a rapidly growing revivalist Hindu movement. Vishnu Das fully supported his decision.

'This is what our country needs. Disciplined and dedicated young men forging a strong nation that does not ape the West. A male nation! No more of that irrational emotionalism which has sapped our energy over centuries. Your father would have been proud of you!'

Deserted by Vivek, Baba's disciples, unlike those of many other gurus, never banded together in a sect that would perpetuate his memory or message. The spiritual seeds planted by Baba' initiation did not take visible root. All that remains of those days is a framed portrait of Baba on one of the walls in the inner sanctum of the Sitaram temple. Commissioned by the Dhamani family and done in garish poster colours by a painter of cinema hoardings, it shows

Baba, with impossibly ruby-red lips and the rosy cheeks of a film star, sitting cross-legged on a tiger skin in the manner of an ancient sage, his right hand raised in benediction. At the top of the painting, against the background of an improbably blue sky, bejewelled figures of Rama and Sita are benevolently looking down at him, a shower of petals falling in blessing from goddess Sita's cupped hands. Baba's boys, now middle-aged men immersed in their family and professional lives, try to visit the temple at least once a week when they place fresh flowers under the portrait.

Even though he was a latecomer, Vivek now occupies one of the top positions in the Sangh's hierarchy where he is rumoured to be a key figure in the organization's think tank which is responsible for chalking out campaigns and strategies for spreading a Hindu ethos in the country's social and cultural life. He has never married and after the death of his mother in 1990 (his grand-uncle and grand-aunt passed away within a month of each other in 1982), he now lives in his one-room office in Johri bazaar, sleeping at night on a mattress spread on the floor. He is widely admired within the Sangh for his ascetic lifestyle though people have wondered about his attachment to a small bronze statue that stands on the window sill of his office and which he always takes with him on his travels around the country. It is the statue of Ram-lalla. Once in a while, he awakens from a dream he can never remember with an acute sensation of loss sobbing through his chest. Coils of despair seem to tighten around his heart as he comes fully awake, making him gasp for breath. These are feelings utterly foreign to his busy life with which he is fully satisfied and which he believes is ennobled by dedication to a sacred cause. For a couple of minutes, his eyes are involuntarily drawn to the statue of child Rama silhouetted by the dim yellow street light coming in through the glass panes of the window. A wave of longing, another unfamiliar emotion, washes over him as he tries to sink back into sleep. He knows Ram-lalla will never move again.

Afterword

MANY INCIDENTS IN Gopal's story are based on events in the life of the great Bengali mystic, Ramakrishna Paramahamsa (1836–1886). Vivek's childhood and youth have a number of parallels with those of Ramakrishna's chosen successor, Swami Vivekananda (1863–1902). Yet both Gopal and Vivek are fictional characters, not to be confused with the real life saint and his heroic disciple. Accounts of many other mystics, notably Muktananda, Gopikrishna, Ramana Maharishi and Teresa of Avilla were invaluable for he descriptions of Gopal's spiritual states. I owe a debt of gratitude to many poets, especially those with a mystical bent—Surdas, Tukaram, Gerard Manley Hopkins, Rainer Maria Rilke, Theodor Roethke, Elizabeth Jennings—whose works provided some of the images with which I have tried to enter the heart of the 'ineffable'. For though I respect and am moved by the mystic's concerns, I am far from being one myself and this can only echo Michel de Certeau's confession in the Introduction to his book *La Fable Mystique*: 'Ce livre se présente au nom d'une incompétence: it est exilé de ce quil traite' 'This book presents itself in the name of incompetence: it is exiled from that which it treats').

I am grateful to David Davidar, Ravi Singh, Christine Zeile, Georges Borchardt and especially my wife, Katha, for their comments and suggestions.